AMERICAN SYCAMORE

To Fran, Annie and Jacob

AMERICAN SYCAMORE

Karen Fielding

Seren is the book imprint of
Poetry Wales Press Ltd
57 Nolton Street, Bridgend, Wales, CF31 3AE
www.serenbooks.com
Facebook: facebook.com/SerenBooks
Twitter: @SerenBooks

ISBN: 978-1-78172-117-9
Kindle: 978-1-78172-139-1
Ebook: 978-1-78172-138-4

Cover image: Neil Robinson
Typesetting by Elaine Sharples
Printed by Bell and Bain, Glasgow

The publisher works with the financial assistance of
The Welsh Books Council

All this happened, more or less.

Slaughterhouse 5, Kurt Vonnegut

For my brother

PART I

NORTH OF
THE MASON DIXON LINE

ABOUT BEFORE

I have yet to see a bear walk in the woods. I have not seen anyone struck by lightning or drown in the river. But these things happen. They always do and they always will and Billy Sycamore, two years older, two foot taller, and too good a fisherman to notice much, got a little funny. Sometimes people ask if I have a brother. This is a perfectly normal question. I'm just not sure how to reply.

The great cities of the world built themselves upon the great rivers of the world. People need the rivers, not vice versa. People forget that. Some rivers start from snows high up or springs underground. Some crisscross each other; some roar along steady and strong. Some disappear.

People used to think the Susquehanna River, like all great rivers encircling the globe, magically flowed from the middle of the earth. That's what people thought when the world was still flat.

Lately I have been thinking about my own beginnings along the Susquehanna River with its hundreds of rivulets and tributaries converging.

I am lonely for this river.

The home with black shutters and large-winged crows. The red geraniums in summer and horse chestnuts in the fall. The abandoned old house by the creek.

The fish in the woods that walked to the river.

The Indian who flew away like a bird.

MRS SPRAGUE

When the river rose and flooded our town the wind blew the geography teacher's roof off. She lived in a tin-clad house close to the Susquehanna River. There were lightning rods jutting from the roof in various angles and directions, much like the hair that sprung out from Mrs Sprague's head. In 1972 Mrs Sprague wore cat-shaped eyeglasses and she hated the North Vietnamese. She despised them in the same way a preacher hates the Devil. On the other hand, she seemed to like Richard Nixon and Germany was pretty high on her list too. She made us learn the days of the week in German. She made us count to twenty in German. Then she'd tell us the North Vietnamese were going into South Vietnam to kill all those poor people. She made it sound pretty dire, Mrs Sprague. Then she'd have us write on a piece of paper if we were for the North Vietnamese or the South Vietnamese. After a manipulative speech like that, who in their right mind is going to write down 'North Vietnamese' unless their parents made their own peanut butter or grew pot in their backyard. Nobody in our seventh-grade class had any more enlightened parental types than we had – upper middle class drunks who voted for Richard Nixon, twice.

I remember glancing up from my desk to see her unfold each piece of paper and nod her head with the satisfaction of a mongoose. And I remember when she asked if Billy Sycamore was my brother. 'Are you related?'

'He's my brother,' I said.

'Well that's very odd,' she said. 'When I asked if you were his sister he said: "Mrs Sprague, we aren't related at all."'

THE REAL PEOPLE

Along the banks of the Susquehanna River the ancient bones of Indian chiefs were buried with strings of beads, a couple of spears, and a few clay pots.

Each year we had a spring thaw. If it melted too much snow on the Blue Ridge Mountains, it churned up the banks and shifted the bones of the Indians, while the floodwater trapped whitetail deer and black bears on chunks of ice in the fast-flowing river.

For some time, the bears had been lumbering into town, across the Lincoln Avenue Bridge, along Union Street, and into the yards of the houses higher on the hilltop looking for food for themselves and their cubs. A black bear standing seven foot tall broke into a house. It tore a hole right through the wire mesh of the screened-in porch. It had smelled peanut butter cookies cooling on a tray. The bear sat down on an Oriental rug and ate all two dozen cookies. Then it did a crap in the middle of the rug and went home.

They say our great great grandfather ran like hell when he saw a black bear. He migrated to North America from Wales in 1760 and he arrived with a cane fishing rod and hand-tied flies. He drank too much, and he spoke Welsh when he drank too much, telling anyone who would listen that the Spanish were not the first explorers to set foot in the new world, it was the Welsh.

He fished the streams feeding the Susquehanna River flowing east, to the sea, those tributaries on the western side running downstream. He spent his whole lifetime on the river. He met the Iroquois people there. He spoke to them in Welsh and they gave him chewing gum. Star-shaped leaves, winged twigs and spiny seed balls. Sweet gum sap.

The Iroquois people must have liked our great great grandfather. They didn't scalp him.

They might have said: 'See this stream? One day it won't meander through the mayflower and dogwood and pine. It's going to shift and the water won't act right anymore. It will be put upon. When things are put upon, they don't act right.'

YELLOW BREECHES CREEK

Billy Sycamore wore a vest with twenty-seven pockets. It was regulation khaki and he kept all sorts of things in there: a can of Pepsi, a .38 caliber pistol, his math homework. He had saved up a lot of birthday money to buy the gun.

The Terry twins, identical fair-haired sisters who would grow into the well-earned titles 'Herpes I' and 'Herpes II', liked to hang out by the river. They tried to seem adept at bait and tackle. They tried to seem knowledgeable about the fathead minnow and the rainbow smelt. They did all of this fishing fabrication to impress Billy because Billy was most handsome: eyes the colour of river algae, and black lashes like the long, evening shadows in a mountain stream. His dusky blond hair grew into a wild curly haze. He had a smile that was infectious but uneven; when he turned fourteen he removed his braces with a wrench.

On his fifteenth birthday the twins gave Billy a lighter. Well-polished brass with a flintlock and tiny wheel. Billy said they shoplifted it.

Billy liked the sisters and he liked the lighter. He said he'd keep it in one of his pockets should he ever have to face a firing squad.

There are no firing squads in south central Pennsylvania, so Billy and I used the lighter to set off firecrackers in the field behind our house instead. A great whirl of flame, wheat, and scorched summer grass rose into the sky. The blowback caught the edge of his T-shirt forcing him to the ground to roll over the crickets and grasshoppers and wild strawberries beneath him. But he liked to spend the majority of his time fishing. Not because the twins sat either side of him – mostly without their clothes on – but because the waist-deep waters of Yellow

Breeches Creek and the cool, fast-flowing current tugged at his heart and fishing line.

Billy stood barefoot in the cold mountain stream. He'd dead-drift a white belly sculpin or dry-fly fish using woolly buggers. Now and then he used Wonder bread and Velveeta cheese. He did a lot of dry-fly fishing in late summer when the trout feed on the surface of the creek. He fished the upper end of the creek where the stream narrowed to twenty feet in places, until the river changed again. When it flowed eastward it widened and took a shot of cold water from Boiling Springs Lake.

Sometimes his friend Juan Goldstein came along. The Ludwig Wittgenstein of our little town, Juan could relate to Billy in parallelograms. His IQ was way up there. He was also a philosopher. When Juan's grandparents died during an earthquake in Mexico City (a building fell on them) he said, 'Ah, yes. But they were old.'

Billy held the unwavering respect of Juan, for his original way of seeing reality and for never failing to have, on hand, a reliable source of inspiration and justification.

> *Nuestra vidas son los rios*
> *Que van a dar en el mar*

He started thinking laterally, Billy, which is not a good thing for somebody who walks into a room and says, 'I'm going to kill myself today, and what are you doing?'

> *que es el morir…*[1]

Try as I might, I could not see the connection between butane and one's own soul except when Billy and Juan tried to set my hair on fire.

14

which is death...

Billy rowed along the ever-drifting memory bank of his mind. He tried to forget and he tried to remember. He ran his fingers along the edges of life: leaves toothed and lobed, or arranged feather-like; needle-like. He seemed clear-eyed, truer to the curve of his own life with a fishing rod than at any other time, unaware of what was going to come his way.

AMERICAN ANGLER

Everything affects me. Everything affected Billy too.

We come from a long line of affected people.

Our Great Aunt Belle thought she was a lumberjack. She walked the streets of a little coalmining town in northeast Pennsylvania in the deep snows at Christmas, carrying an axe and sizing up trees. Then she'd wander down to the railroad tracks, drink whisky with the dirty old men she let fondle her breasts. Our mother's family made money in hotels along the Susquehanna River, then in soda pop. Then they had Aunt Belle's frontal lobe removed.

Some said Billy was beautiful but wild like a river when it floods its banks. 'He's like Aunt Belle,' they'd whisper. Aunt Belle had the lobotomy; nobody wanted to be like her. 'I think he takes after Great Aunt Elvira,' said somebody else. Great Aunt Elvira wore men's clothes and she could do five different types of dog barks. Nobody wanted to be like her.

Billy said the Sycamore was the tree whose leaf most closely resembled the human heart. For his eighth birthday our father offered him a heart: a human heart made out of plastic. It had ventricles, four chambers, and blue-and-red-coloured veins. Our father hoped Billy would become a doctor like both he and his father before him. He wanted Billy to have direction. The heart sat on his dresser until he turned twelve, got a BB gun and blew a hole through it.

Billy's own heart took shape in the mountains. On a freezing night in a tent pitched beneath a black sky filled with silver stars, when our parents ran off and married.

Sometimes I tried to picture my mother, an eighteen year old, dark hair streaming down and her shoes crushing the tightly curled heads of ferns; a wind blowing across her mouth like sails on a ship carrying strangers to distant places; but she was anchored here, where the stillness and fury had astonished her: flame-rose cheeks and lilac-blue eyes, hands to thighs, mud-caked conscience. She said she could smell the sea and taste the salt on her tongue. But this was the river, where filtered light bathes tree roots, touches the earth… it was mid-winter after all; the earth was rain-soaked and snowy, full of decaying leaves.

When Billy turned nine our father gave him a chemistry set. Billy mixed water, ethanol and Red Dye Number 2, and convinced me it was an alchemical recipe for grape juice. I took a sip then blacked out for forty-five minutes. It was pretty obvious to me he was about as medically inclined as our dog, Marvin.

But still what Billy loved most was fishing. His heart and chemical make-up belonged to the river, the current, and flow; the behaviour of fish; and technically he excelled at fly-casting and fly-fishing knots. He had subscriptions to *Fly, Rod, & Reel*, *Field & Stream*, *American Angler*, *The Fish Sniffer*, and *Boating World*.

In his tackle box he kept all his hooks and flies. His whole world was chaos except when you opened up his tackle box. I used to slip into his bedroom just to have a look around and fiddle inside the box with its three retractable tiers, shiny lures, and plastic beads with painted eyes and wearing tiny grass skirts. He organised his lead weights, metal hooks, and rolls of tackle in various stages of exactitude.

He talked a lot about his fishing adventures, but he rarely took me. He talked about the cold, clear streams and creeks that overflowed when it rained too hard.

He talked about pike, pickerel, trout, and bass, like they were beautiful flowers in bloom. He became knowledgeable about the secret ways of minnow, grayling and trout. He understood lures, jigs, spoons and spinners better than he understood himself. He could talk about fishing until the sun set behind the Blue Ridge Mountains, and the fish sank into the darkness of the water below him; and he'd continue to cast and re-cast his line until the stars rose between his outstretched arms.

Billy Sycamore may have sat perplexed in a world of possibility but it had nothing to do with his birth or bloodline. I maintain it had everything to do with what occurred a few months before his thirteenth birthday – one March afternoon when he'd gone down to the river to go fishing – when the heavy spring-time rains drove the trout crazy and pushed them out of their winter hidey-holes. He burst through the door at home dripping with agitation and river mud. Stinking of gunpowder, scratched up and blood dried, he fled down to the basement and refused to come up. Our parents figured this was normal adolescent behaviour: sulky and withdrawn. We nearly collided in front of the basement stairs.

'What's wrong with you?' I asked. He looked breathless and wild-eyed like Marvin the dog after chasing a cat down Canton Street. I searched for traces of foam at the corners of my brother's mouth.

'Nothing. What's wrong with *you*?'

Billy's usual reply. He turned everything around to get around everything.

He also started to read the thesaurus for amusement. He'd say things like: 'I'm feeling hyperborean' when he meant 'distant', or 'hypothetical' when he caught a cold. He began to think about everything more and mostly in the wrong direction. He seemed put upon. Like a stream that didn't meander right.

HOW TO COOK A RACCOON

Union Street is a two-lane road that runs mostly downstream with the current of the river. It can also run upstream all the way past Thurmont. On this route is the Indian Trading Post. The Indian Trading Post sold handmade maple-walnut candy and books on how to cook a raccoon. Billy liked the Indian Trading Post. He liked to read the pamphlets on how not to get struck by lightning (take your golf shoes off first, *then* run) and how to avoid an angry bear (play dead, *then* run).

One fine July afternoon, before Billy began glancing behind him or around the next corner – he'd go down to the Indian Trading Post to read-up on death-by-black eastern bear. He'd traipse through the cool and leafy back woods shortcut leading down to the river then halt abruptly on a lengthy stretch of asphalt.

'What's wrong?' I asked. Sometimes he let me tag along. Today was one of those days.

'I don't feel like walking anymore,' he said.

As children we were told to run away if a car stopped and the driver asked for directions, and never to accept candy from a stranger; we weren't even allowed to take a ride from people we knew.

'What if it's Mrs Kelman?' we asked. Mrs Kelman was about ninety years old and lived behind us in a stone house with a Great Dane. The Great Dane and I will become acquainted so well the police will have to shoot it.

'Nobody,' said our mother. And she made us swear up and down to high holy heaven we would never hitchhike.

Our town, like a lot of towns everywhere, attracted all kinds. John the Baptist appeared to a man and his wife ten miles upstream and told them the Susquehanna River was good for washing away sins. Geronimo rode a horse down Union Street on his way to Washington DC to meet Teddy Roosevelt and the President of Swingers of America managed Buzzy's Italian next to the bank on Stevenson Avenue.

We have UFOs. They are hiding-out in the abandoned coal shafts in the western part of the state zipping in and out of the entrance at impossible angularity. During Billy's thesaurus phase he'd refer to their manoeuvering as *V-shaped obliquity*.

Now we were standing in the hot July wind hitchhiking. About twenty cars had whizzed past in the last half hour when a black Studebaker came lumbering toward us like an old black bear and grumbled to a stop. A man with a bowl haircut and acne scars leaned across the seat and smiled through the window: 'Where you goin'?'

'The Indian Trading Post,' said Billy.

The door nearly fell off when he kicked it open. 'Hop in,' he said.

Billy tried to climb into the backseat but there was no backseat to climb into.

'Seat's in the shop so you can squeeze in front with me,' said the man, pitching the brown paper bag next to him onto the floor. The man shoved it aside with his foot and several empty beer cans rolled out. 'Now there's room,' he said.

Billy started to get in when the man stopped him – 'stick her in the middle.'

I didn't want to get in the man's car.

'She gets car sick,' said Billy. 'She has to sit next to a window.'

'Aw, she won't git car sick,' said the man. 'I ain't driving you to Maine.'

We weren't even allowed to keep the apples that people handed-out for Halloween. Even the judge up the street wasn't exempt in case this year he happened to slide razor blades in the apples like good sociopaths do every Halloween in America.

We'd all seen the instructional film. Mandatory viewing from the fourth grade on – where a stranger tells a little girl he's got some candy in his car.

'I've got some candy in my car. You like candy?'

'Sure I do,' says the little girl.

Of course the last scene is her lone sneaker floating down a creek somewhere in the woods, anywhere and everywhere. It's pretty obvious the pervert did something sick and unforgiving to the child.

The man is staring at me. 'Hey, tutti frutti,' he asks with a derisive little smirk – 'you like candy?' The question turned out to be exceptionally motivational because I sprinted all the way to Union Street and Saint Claire Avenue. I didn't want to get chopped up and buried in bits and pieces in the woods like that hunter from West Pittston last autumn whose heart was roasted over a fire by an escapee from the State Hospital. Or left rotting under a snowdrift like that poor woman a few winters back whose skeleton was discovered in the quietly melting heap with an eight-month-old skeleton baby inside her ribcage. Both stabbed by some maniac with a screwdriver.

By dinnertime Billy turned up with a Hershey Bar.

'He really did have candy,' said Billy.

So it seemed just plain hypocritical one afternoon as a seven-year old, sitting at Woolworths luncheon counter that the man occupying the stool next to me, a fat slob in a boiler suit, was allowed to pat my pigtails. 'Ain't you the cutest little pie? Ain't you got a smile for Ole Dickie?'

I did not have a smile for old Dickie. I had nothing but a bad feeling in my whole circulatory system for Dickie. I knew

21

nothing could happen, though, because on the other side of me sat my mother. However, I also knew her presence did not guarantee a thing as four years earlier she stood with me at the bottom of the Kelman's driveway, chatting away to Mrs Kelman about this and about that when the Kelman's Great Dane mistook me for a muskrat and tore half my face off. Both women managed to yank the dog off, however neither was sure I still had my right eye anymore. I knew when I saw that dog thundering down the driveway it was gunning for me, as sure as I knew Ole Dickie wanted to do unthinkable things to me now.

I looked at my mother who was looking at herself in a beautifully wrought sterling silver hand-held mirror she'd fished out of her camel-leather handbag. She pushed her eyebrows up with her pinkie finger. She pulled down at her dark, teased hair. She applied a brick-red lipstick from a gold metal tube.

And now, after all the warnings, set like so many mental rat traps about perverts, strangers, and the like I hear her say: 'Go on – *be mannerly.*'

I thought she was well and truly crazy.

Of course her comment only encouraged the man. He started rubbing the sides of his face and the tops of his huge thighs. He was all jumpy and excited like it was Christmas time in paedophileville. He asked if I liked milkshakes. Did I play Jacks? – He bet I liked strawberry shortcake! He had a whole stack of colouring books in his truck – would I like to choose one? I looked over at my mother who was blotting her lips on a paper napkin while I was being pumped for personal details and groomed for child abduction. I stared into the stainless-steel countertop. Everything smelled of disinfectant.

The waitress stopped by. She distracted the man with the banana split he now probably regretted ordering.

22

But as we got up to go, he grabbed my elbow.

'You gonna give Dickie a little kiss?' he asked me. 'That'd make Dickie happy 'cause Dickie been real sad lately.' He made an exaggerated frown. He also pushed his face so close to mine I could see the chocolate syrup filling the gaps in his molars dripping onto his tongue, dark rivulets in a stream. He spat out a coin – a silver dime onto the countertop, spinning then stopping with an abrupt clatter when he smacked his hand flat on top of it.

'For the ferryman,' he said.

GENERAL LEE

My name is Alice Sycamore. I don't have a nickname.

'Hey, Alice,' people say.

'Hey,' I say.

My middle name is Lee. Our father says we are related to General Robert E. Lee, which is a huge and ridiculous lie. We are about as related to Robert E. Lee as we are to a raccoon.

We live along the southeastern curve of the Susquehanna River where the Broadway Limited barrels along the old forged iron tracks between New York City and Chicago blowing anthracite into the atmosphere – a beautiful shiny lump of high-density coal discovered by a man who accidentally set fire to a mountain. There were Indian people too, and the slaves running north and Union soldiers running south, everybody coming or going, passing through, doing whatever people do in their time and place. At least I thought so then, or remember it that way. Of course memory can be subjective. Except I remember everything, even other people's memories, in particular the ones they want to forget like when the Prom Queen told me my family was sick.

'Your family is sick,' she said.

The Prom Queen can go fuck herself (I mean that in the nicest way, of course) and I like to think of the Sycamores as rugged individualists: us and Theodore Roosevelt. This comparison to Teddy Roosevelt made our father as happy as a worm in a Tequila bottle.

'You're a rugged individualist,' I told my father, 'you and Theodore Roosevelt.'

'Indeed!' he said. 'Let's go pick pineapples!'

There are no pineapples in Pennsylvania, and the Prom Queen's brother will move to Belize where he will live with a group of people who make their own peanut butter. But before this he got a pet monkey. I liked to go to their house to see the monkey. The monkey's name was Chester and it lived in a large wire cage in the basement of their colonial white-brick home.

It was all alone down there, the monkey. It had a water pistol to play with which it had thrown to the bottom of the cage.

I read that 99.9 per cent of pet monkeys are mentally disturbed. I have met a lot of people 99.9 per cent disturbed. The monkey chirped like a sparrow. He rubbed his black hands together like a neurotic French sea captain.

After a while, as with most new and exciting things, the monkey's novelty wore off: nobody came downstairs to visit the monkey; people stopped paying attention to it. The Prom Queen's brother threw peanuts at it. The only friendly face was the cleaning lady. She'd scream: HELLO MONKEY, then wring out her mop.

The monkey escaped from the basement. It climbed through an open window and ran up a buttonwood also known as a plane or sycamore tree and this tree was as good and familiar as anything it may have ever swung around on in the Ecuadorian jungle. It yanked off one-inch brown pods and threw them at the sidewalk. It threw them at parked and moving cars. It hurtled them down on the small crowd gathering. One hit a man on the head; another struck a woman in her face. The monkey was the happiest it had been in its whole life until a squirrel bit its tail.

One day the monkey's house will be swallowed by river water. The house will fill with the rising muddy tide from the great spring rains that made the Susquehanna River swell from the mouth of the Chemung River all the way to the Chesapeake Bay. But nobody will remember the monkey.

The president of the United States, who would nearly get impeached for monkey business of his own, flew along the great jagged spine of the river to see just what mischief the Susquehanna had gotten up to. His helicopter landed on the roof of a local high school.

He got out and grinned at the people. He waved at the people. He made comments about the power and destruction of river water. Then he got back into his helicopter and flew away into the great sky, far from the whorl of the town sinking below him.

THE SEVENTH STREET
BILLIARD HALL

Our house was struck by lightning more than flooded by water. The bolts shook the earth; shut the electricity off. The wind blew hard and bent the great spruce pines. We all knew what was coming, what we were in for. The kind of storm that transformed the sky, coloured it – dense purple and black, like nausea. I have always been afraid of the dark and I don't like lightning. Even now the dark presses in on me and lightning can rattle my soul. Of course Billy didn't mind either one. He liked the dark. He thought about the electric chair. He could sit in a canoe on the river fishing while lightning struck all around him.

'You weren't worried?' I asked.

'Worried about what?' he said.

When we were children we were sent to the local day camp. Billy waited until all the other kids filed inside the old yellow-brick building by the river, then he'd take the downtown bus to the Seventh Street Billiard Hall where he'd shoot pool with all the blacks and whites on welfare.

He got away with this until the day camp called our parents asking if Billy had had his spleen removed as he had instructed somebody to tell one of the camp's staff.

By the time he was eleven Billy hung around by the old fort on the river. A great house made of fieldstone with wide shutters, an outhouse, and an old well. In its grander days the house kept out Indians and Confederate soldiers. It hid slaves running away from southern farms and plantations.

In the grounds rose a huge buttonwood tree he'd climb. Billy said he could see things from the top. He'd stay up there watching the snow stop falling and the stars come out. He followed the confluence of the muddy water and the small islands scattered in the river and the souls of the dead lighting fires. Billy saw the lost and forgotten Indian chiefs walking around the Susquehanna River Valley to the Ohio River and all the way to the Great Lakes and even further north, to Canada.

Down here, he said, they sit on Halfway Island and watch people get off the old paddlewheel ferry at Crows Landing. But the people don't notice them. The people are in their own worlds, occupied by their own ideas. There's plenty happening between heaven and earth but nobody pays much attention to what's around them, so the Indians shrug and move on. They might catch minnows in a soda bottle on the shores of the Chesapeake. They might pull whiskers out of their chin with clam shells.

Billy talked about French troops in blue uniforms and English soldiers in red. He saw black slaves with impossible irons around their ankles and throats, running towards Philadelphia. He saw the fish in the river: the rock bass and pickerel, walleye and trout.

He saw the Susquehannock people walking barefoot. They walked along the same path the joggers will use and street performers and kids with handguns. Then they turned away from the river, the Indian people, and walked into the wooded hills. They passed the Country Club, Pumpkin World USA, Gail's Nail Mart, the Bullet Barn, and sixteen thousand different churches. They continued along to a concrete dam. Then they very kindly left a couple of arrowheads for Billy and me to find three thousand years later.

DICK'S WORLD OF POWER TOOLS

In those earliest years, long gone to me now, a lot of quality time was spent in Dick's World of Power Tools. Our dad loved Dick's. He loved it like a strange first cousin. He was there so often, buying drill bits and hand tools, the clerk used to ask him: 'You wanna use your employee discount for those?'

Our dad preferred slacks to trousers. He liked Perma Press. He liked Wash N Wear. He did flared. Yet he wouldn't touch a paisley neckerchief with a twenty-foot fishing pole. He had Billy and me stand in front of the dryer while he took out one of his Perma Press shirts. He gave it a flap and said, 'See this? Now *this* is progress.'

One day our father vanished. Just like the Monongahela Indians. They had disappeared off the face of earth. By the early seventeenth century they were gone. The whole world was empty of the Monongahela Indians. They left no trail.

Just before six o'clock on an overcast and muggy summer evening in 1969, waiting for an electrical storm to rage through Barnard Township like a wild pack of snapping hounds, our father should have been sitting at the dinner table, stabbing at his bowl of iceberg lettuce and complaining about his boss: 'Just because a man's in a wheelchair doesn't mean he's not a bastard – pass the blue cheese.' Now our mother kept glancing over at his empty plate.

The wind spat tree branches at our glass windows and in the distance a rumble of thunder coming from Thurmont bellowed through the darkening sky and I felt on edge like animals in the woods might feel; every nerve tingling before a storm – yet they know how to run for cover. But I was here – seated at the dinner table watching my mother's suntanned and freckled pretty face take on that wildwoman worried look which always preceded over-reaction escalating to an apocalyptic sense of doom.

Over the years our father must have come up with some doozies to calm our mother, who tended to worry in disproportion to an event: Like now he's twenty minutes late so he's probably been hit by a cement truck.

She looked at us. 'Did your father call today and you forgot to tell me?'

I thought about this for a moment. I didn't want to be thinking about a missing father. I wanted to think about *Gilligan's Island*.

Our father liked *Gilligan's Island*. He liked to wolf-whistle at Ginger.

'He's been kidnapped by a Japanese submariner,' I said.

'You watch too much TV,' said our mother.

She even owned one of the dresses Marianne wore on an episode: A sleeveless pink gingham print with a huge white daisy on the left pocket. The Lacey sisters liked to come over and look at The Marianne Dress in our mother's closet. Then we'd all try the dress on and get a big kick out of it.

'Maybe he stopped off to buy another pine tree,' said Billy. Last week our father came home with four blue spruces strapped to the top of his Buick. He couldn't wait to get out a shovel and start digging.

'Perhaps,' said our mother. Then she glanced at her wristwatch. A delicate gold one with seed pearls around the face. 'It's after six,' she said.

'So?' said Billy.

'Sears is closed.'

Our mother got up from the table to call the hospital where our father worked. We could hear her voice breaking, full of concern: 'Could you page Doctor Sycamore *again*, please?'

After several minutes she'd return to the table looking crazier than before. She was beautiful, our mother; an extrovert yet flammable, a walking can of gasoline just waiting for a match.

The blackening sky and increasing winds seemed to keep pace with the crescendo of events but for the moment I was preoccupied by the streaks of lightning I could see over the Blue Ridge Mountains, breaking up the sky.

'Maybe he's been shipwrecked,' I said.

By 6.30pm the storm broke upon us, illuminating the sky with flashes of light followed by the powerful heart-stopping explosions of thunder. The rain pounded the pitched roof of the house, slashing against the windows, while strong gusts of wind shook the big black shutters. One must have come loose because it was banging against the house.

Our mother would not let us turn on the television 'in case it blew up' she said. We weren't allowed to use the phone 'in case an electrical current came through the earpiece and set our hair on fire'. And most of all we could not open a window – not even a crack – in case the lightning caught the edge of a rug or a sofa, starting a house fire, or worse, decapitating one of us like it did that poor elderly man asleep in his bed next to a wide-open window in Danville last summer.

We had to sit in the dark, not intentionally, but because all the power had been knocked out, including the telephone now – and nobody could remember where the candles were.

'Your father must have gotten caught in the storm. A flat tyre,' she said. And she brightened at the thought as if this is what had happened and now we could all eat the ice cream melting in the freezer.

But by 9pm when the power came back on and the telephone worked and the whole neighbourhood was cooled-off and dripping and still no sign of our father, our mother called the hospital and spoke to the late shift operator who said: *Dr Sycamore is not on call tonight.*

Our mother called the Barnard Township Police Department now. The Barnard Township Police Department informed her that missing for three hours is not justification for a manhunt with sniffer dogs.

'But you do have bloodhounds?' our mother asked. 'Don't they need to go out?'

The Barnard Township Police told our mother she would have to wait until 6pm the following evening to file a missing persons report.

Between 9 and 10pm she was on the horn calling everybody and anybody asking if they'd seen our father and everybody and anybody said: *Haven't seen him.*

By 11pm our mother's teary-eyed and mascara-stained face looked both beautiful and tragic.

By midnight our mother made us go to bed. 'He'll be home when you wake up,' she tried to sound confident but by now I wasn't so sure we'd ever see him again and the thought of it made me burst into tears.

Billy put his hand on my shoulder. 'Don't worry Alice. Dad's okay. You'll see.'

However when I got up the next morning at 6am I found a frazzled and red-eyed mother who had already contacted the Pennsylvania Department of Transportation, the FBI, and the Barnard County Snow Removal, even though it was late July.

By 7.30am Opal Pike, who cleaned our house, turned up ready to mop and when told about our missing father, she said, 'Nothing don't happen for nothing.'

Billy said our dad had been kidnapped by a flying saucer.

This was around the time the man from Snowflake, Arizona had been abducted for five days before the aliens dropped him off at a gas station.

'He was okay though, wasn't he?' our mother asked. Obviously she didn't read the same newspapers as Billy.

'Well, no,' said Billy.

Then, unlike the Monongahela Indians, our father reappeared. At 8.35am the Barnard County Police Department called to confirm our father had left his car parked in a motel upriver.

He'd been missing for fifteen and one half hours and found propped against some sweet, young saplings, the kind the Monongahela used to build their beehive-shaped houses. They would drive the trees into the ground in a twenty-foot-wide circle, bent and lashed the tops together. They covered the frame in tree bark and mats woven from catty nine tails. They boiled everything and they ate with spoons made from elk antlers.

If the Amerindians Indians believed in interstellar people there is no recorded evidence on their pottery or bone ornaments. They left a few ancient rock paintings of walking fish on the empty islands rising out of the middle of the river.

By 9.05am the police called back to say our father had been discovered by a dog walker. This was a blessing as he really liked dogs. And according to the dog walker's account *he looked dead, but wasn't; like an insect playing dead, but isn't.* The dog walker poked him with a stick.

'Hey, are you alright? Is anybody home?'

Our whole universe tilted that day. Not because our father was dead, but because he wasn't. 'Almost, but God gave him back,' that's what our mother said.

'God didn't want him,' that's what Opal Pike said.

The police told our mother, based on physical evidence:

scorch marks on his hands, the fact the eyelets on his shoes had melted, and the loose coins in his pocket had smelted into one lump sum, he'd most likely been struck by lightning.

Our father could not recall what he was doing in the woods. Nor could he recall why his car was parked at the motel. But there are no mysteries. There are reasons for things.

'What were you doing at the motel?' asked our mother.

'What motel?' said our father. He was wearing a bandage diagonally across his head.

'The Bluebird Motel.'

Opal came through just then with a hand sweeper. 'That motel's for the lustful and indecent,' she said.

'Please say you aren't lustful and indecent,' said our mother, her hands pressed against her chest as if she was trying to keep her heart from breaking.

'If I was I can't remember,' said our father.

'Well what *do* you remember?' Our mother asked him.

'Everything but that,' he said.

The human mind can grasp, but not always fathom, even when it's right in front of a person's nose like a flying saucer – or a double-crossing husband; but after the lightning bolt our father sat around a lot in our mother's pink robe watching re-runs of *Gilligan's Island*.

BUFFALO HOOF

Opal Pike lived downriver in Milroy. She suffered an ingrown toenail. She'd hobble around our house with it wrapped up in ten layers of gauze and seeping through with blood. Her dark oily hair kinked down her neck in wiry braids and stayed caught up like a thick rattlesnake in a hairnet. She wore turquoise and silver, heavy rings and bracelets. She clanked all the time.

'That bastard doctor hurt like *hell*. He yanked my whole nail off so you tell your mama I'm moving real slow today,' she'd say, spit over her shoulder, and carry herself like an ancient mountain around the kitchen.

She'd been working for our family since the spring of 1964, when our mother put a help wanted ad in the local newspaper, answered by a woman whose front teeth were gone. 'Got knocked out in a fight,' she'd say and poke a finger through the dark space in her mouth. She was a God-fearing, churchgoing woman with five children and a husband dying from advanced diabetes who drove her to our house every day in a big gold Cadillac.

Everybody liked her but the dog didn't.

'That dog don't like coloured people,' she said.

That was 1964.

'That dog don't like negro people,' she said.

That was 1966.

'That dog don't like blacks,' she said.

That was 1968.

She said 'nigger' in between them all.

She called Billy a 'wild little nigger'.

'Ain't he white?' I said.

'So, what?' she said.

Sometimes we sat around doing nothing while she mopped the yellow linoleum floor in our kitchen. She'd talk to us like we weren't really five and seven years old respectively, but more like equals. She drank strong black coffee with ten teaspoons of sugar. Sometimes she'd give us a sip. Then she'd stare out the kitchen window above the double stainless steel sink and read the sky. 'That cloud looks like a copperhead. The one behind it looks like a weasel.' Then she'd mutter something about a bad spirit or the Great Spirit – and then to distance herself from whatever they were, she liked to unravel the bandage on her toe and show us.

Opal was brought up along the old Lackawanna Indian trail. Those trails were pounded out along the tributaries, creeks, and streams that seemed to flow from her eyes and fingertips whenever she got to talking about her upbringing along a bend of the Susquehanna River's northern branch, a place that had built itself up around the downtown that begins and ends on Railroad Avenue. She described two-storey wood-clad houses knuckled down in concrete and perched on a hilltop. It all overlooked the Susquehanna, flowing faintly in the drought of summertime, like the fossilised remains of a real river pulled through the broad, steep-sided hills and valleys flanked by rising cliffs, all cut from a glacial past.

It wasn't in the riproaring part of the river, which finds its beginnings in the Tioga Point flowing to its confluence with the Chemung River before filling up the Conewingo Dam. But sometimes Opal said she and her siblings would get an old inner tube from a junkyard and float downstream, past the rocky incline and populated hills, and the depressing metalwork bridge that spanned the length of the river connecting Railroad Avenue.

'I am one quarter Nanticoke,' said Opal – 'related to a great and proud Indian chief named Buffalo Hoof.'

'You don't look Indian,' said Billy.

'If I is lyin' deliver a bolt of lightning and set me alight, Lord,' said Opal.

Billy waited about two minutes for her very large head to combust but it didn't so he said, 'Alright,' but he never believed her, even though she threw around Native American sayings like: 'I'm digging up the hatchet' when she was feeling forgiving; or 'I'm on the warpath' when she wasn't; or 'Heap Big Fool' referring to our father who tried to exterminate the bagworms in our yard by igniting their bagworm universe with propane gas and a matchstick.

The huge fireball that ensued left him without eyebrows. It also burned down all of the shrubs and bushes growing along the southeast corner of our house.

'We fished a man out of the river,' Opal Pike told me and Billy when there was nothing good on television so her crazy stories filled the gap.

'He must have been happy about that,' I said.

'I don't know if he was happy or not, but he was dead. An' we kept his shoes.'

'Why?'

'They had laces.'

'So?'

'What's the matter with you, girl? Shoes don't come off your feet when they got laces.'

'Did he drown?' asked Billy.

'Bullet,' she held two fingers to her forehead. 'The river flowed straight through him. The shoes were the miracle of him, I reckon.'

'Who shot him?' Billy asked.

'Somebody who didn't much like him,' she said.

'Did they get caught?' he asked.

'Sure they got caught.'

'Did they go to the electric chair?' said Billy.

'Heavens boy – why would the Law stick a white man in the chair for killing a coloured?'

'How d'you know he was white?' he asked.

'How d'you know he weren't?'

Opal said her mother ran a funeral parlour out of their kitchen. Her mother dressed and pickled them. She rubbed rouge into their sallow cheeks and lips, put menthol and pine sap on their tongues. She washed their bodies in Rectifiant. We had no idea about Rectifiant but Opal seemed to know all about it.

We sat around the rosewood table in our kitchen, beneath the open window above the sink where a plum tree burst into pale pink flower in spring and dark purple fruit every summer.

'And she talked to them.'

'Talked to who?'

'The dead people.'

'Didn't she know they were dead?'

'Of course she knew they was dead!'

'Why talk to them then?'

'Why not?' said Opal, as though we were the crazy ones.

'At first I couldn't understand why they wasn't answering her back,' said Opal.

'Didn't they look dead?' Billy asked.

'They looked alright to me,' she said, laughing until her mouth shook like all the pine trees in the world on a windy day. 'We'd eat corn bread dipped in bacon fat. Then mosey to the river and save a few bites to catch some catfish.'

'A funeral don't sound so bad,' said Billy.

'I guess it ain't, if it isn't your own,' she said.

OPAL'S HOUSE

The way Opal talked about being part Nanticoke, Billy figured her family must be living in a wigwam in Milroy. She said her people invented witchcraft. That if they wanted to poison the whole world all they had to do was close their eyes and breathe on it.

Three years and five months before Billy had returned from the woods crazy-eyed and foaming our parents had an emergency. Our uncle, the one with the metal plate in his head, was the emergency – he had suffered a conniption. That's what we were told – 'Your uncle's had a conniption,' followed by, 'so you're going to Opal's house because we can't find a babysitter.'

It was a warm Indian summer Sunday and Billy was instructed to oil his hair and comb the wild curls flat to one side. I had to wear a dress. We knew we looked insane: looking like we were going to church, and we don't even go to church.

From the backseat of the car we watched the large brick houses on Union Street give way to the railroad tracks which gave way to the old pump house then to rusting chain-link fences, run-down looking shops and littered alleys. We entered a neighbourhood with cement-front yards and a mix of single-storey wood bungalows with patched roofs, all vulnerable to the river when it floods its banks.

Our father pulled up to one of the only two-storey brick houses, with a screen door hanging off its hinges. A teenage girl, lanky with tightly woven braids and knee-length shorts on, Opal's eldest child, came over to the car to greet us. Opal was still at church, she explained – The First Baptist of Milroy – but that she'd be home shortly.

The rest of Opal's children hung in a cluster on the porch.

Leaning against the railing, sizing up the honkies. One boy wore a plaid shirt and dark pants too big for him. Another one was trying to tune a transistor radio. Another boy dribbled a half-inflated basketball, the sound made the German shepherd chained up in the yard next door bark. From inside Opal's house I heard a raspy voice shout, 'Shut that damn dog up.'

The boy closest to Billy's age, (with the ill-fitting pants), motioned for Billy to follow him inside and I tagged along. He let the screen door slam. We stood for a moment beneath a waxy fly strip hanging off a light bulb. We followed the boy along a narrow hallway into a small front room. A large round rag rug took up most of the well-scuffed linoleum floor space. The mid-morning sun shone through some old slatted blinds; the pattern of light moving across somebody with calipers on their legs. The person sat half-bent over and about one foot in front of an old black and white television. She had wiry grey and greasy hair pulled back in a tight bun. She was drinking Benadryl cough syrup out of the bottle. She took a sip. Smacked her lips. She looked at me and Billy. She took another sip and asked her grandson without moving her eyes off of us: 'who the *chalkys* be?'

'The Sycamores,' said her grandson. 'You know, Mamma works for them. They needed looking after today.' The grandmother motioned for us to come nearer. We obliged, standing between her and the TV now; she was watching *Manhunt*.

Her eyes burned, two coal fires lit inside her sunken face. Her legs looked like two planks of wood: trees withered, leafless, sapless. Dead a long time.

'You a Baptist?' she asked us.

'No.'

'A Methodist?'

'No.'

'A Heathen?'

We didn't know such a term so we shrugged in a don't-know-but-we-could-be-sort-of-way and her coal eyes flashed – lightning bolts flying across the old rag rug. She wore rings on all her fingers and some settings were empty.

I waited for her to make a fist and strike us down for being heathens.

'You need to be baptized. Or else you goin' to hell when you dead like them.' She whacked the sides of her legs over and over with a metal crutch.

The grandson left her striking at her dead legs. We followed him around his house – like a tour where I ended up in the kitchen. A pair of frilly yellow curtains hung in a window overlooking the chain-link fence and the crazily barking dog next door. Everything smelled like bacon fat and Lysol.

Out back a wash line hung between the chain-link fence and a Great Elm. Some of the kids were staring up at a big grey hornets' nest in the tree. One of Opal's older boys had run an extension cord through the kitchen window and at the other end attached an old Electrolux Vacuum cleaner. It rolled along the earth on broken wheels but the suction appeared to work. He yanked it over to the Great Elm, stood on an upside down vegetable crate and pressed the nozzle against the papery-thin exterior of the hornets' nest dangling between two upper branches of the tree. The nest collapsed like a building set for demolition. It flew straight inside the hosing and into the vacuum bag. The kids were all shouting and swearing and laughing and one of them asked a pretty relevant question: 'Whatchya gonna do with them now?'

The older brother said he was going to stick the vacuum cleaner bag in the freezer. But he left the bag, humming and droning and vibrating on the kitchen table, distracted, as most people are, by something else. A neighbourhood cat slipped through the kitchen window and pounced straight on the bag, sharp claws extended, releasing the hornets to have a wild and retributive party in Opal's wigwam.

The daughter only made them crazier when she sprayed them with Lysol. The hornets dispersed when struck by the cloud of disinfectant then re-grouped into a resentful swarm buzzing out of the kitchen asphyxiated and disoriented deciding to make landfall on the helpless grandmother. The rampaging hornets covered her arms and legs, neck and face, a blanket of sharp thorns and straight pins. 'Get them off me!! – get them off me!! Get the little hornet bastards off me!!' – Her hollering brought the sister running who found the grandmother trying to beat them off with her crutches. But this only incensed and antagonised the hornets who returned to hunt down the poor woman. The stingers tore from their bodies and studded the grandmother's flesh with excruciating pain and poison, while the grandmother waved and flailed her arms and kicked her legs in the air until she fell clean backwards her eyes rolling right up into her skull. Even flat on her back her shouting didn't stop: They stung my eyeballs!! They is stinging my bosom!! I'm dying!!… I'm dying!! Lawd Help Me!! – HELP ME!! Every puncture created a neat red dart surrounded by a sore and swollen wound emerging all over the grandmother until her breathing got ratchety, full of little gasps and intermittent croaking and an ambulance took her to the ER where she was put on a drip.

The older sister grabbed my shoulder and said, 'C'mon.' I traipsed after her up two flights of uneven wooden stairs to a good-sized space below the roof and saw a strange man laid out in a three-piece suit in a wooden box. The air smelled sweet, faintly perfumed.

'Embalming fluid,' she said. Leaning over the dead man she straightened his bow tie.

'He look good, don't he?' I wasn't sure if she wanted to impress the white kid who didn't have a dead man hanging around in her house to play with.

'I guess,' I said. 'He is dead – ain't he?'

'Of course he is!' she looked at me like I was the psycho here.

'Did you kill him?' I asked.

'What?' now she seemed genuinely pissed off.

'Well, how'd he get like that?'

'The sugar took him.'

'He died from sugar?'

'Yep,' she said.

'I have to show Billy,' I said, 'He likes dead things.'

'Oh no you don't,' she said. 'You ain't even s'posed to be up here.'

'Why are we then?'

'We're hiding from those shit-angry bees.'

When Opal came to work Monday she was covered in pink calamine up and down her arms and legs. And her left eye all swelled and sealed shut where her lid got stung. I felt pretty bad for her, but worse for her son, the one who fiddled with the hornets in the first place.

'He stopped feeling the stinging,' said Opal.

'How?' I asked.

'Cause that boy got a whoopin' all the way to Africa and back an' believe you me, it felt worse than any wasp stinging his behind.' Opal said this while slamming her pocketbook

43

down on the kitchen counter about ten times like it was her son's backside.

But she was also distraught about the boa constrictor. The one in the fish tank, in their basement that ate live pink-eyed mice. 'The mice got out! They's all escaped. They's running loose in the house breedin' and carryin' on.' Opal removed a hand-held electric fan from her handbag and whirred it around her face and under her armpits.

Billy listened to Opal's tirade about the mice. He got up from the kitchen table.

Normally such a story would have had him riveted. Instead I found him outside hitting a ball against the side of the house with a tennis racket.

'You let the mice out,' I said.

'No I didn't,' he said.

'Yes you did.' During the destruction of the hornets' nest, Billy stayed behind to inspect the snake. He must have left the latch on the cage door open; he didn't want the poor mice to suffer and die. He also didn't have one wasp sting.

'You don't know anything,' he said. 'They let themselves out.'

GLONELL

That winter Opal Pike's fifth and final child was born. But when the baby arrived she was a disappointment. It is a terrible thing to have a child who is a disappointment; life is not supposed to be that way but it can be.

When the baby got to be five years old Opal would bring her to our house to run wild through it while she cleaned. The baby was named Glonell: she drooled, she wore thick eyeglasses, she was clinically retarded and she liked to play Poker.

A friend of mine, who would one day become a big defence attorney of criminals in Philadelphia, used to come around and she, Billy and I would play cards with Glonell. We'd sit on a Persian rug covering the dark hardwood floor of our den trying not to listen to Glonell exhaling with enormous effort; the hole in her heart, the lack of oxygen to her brain. Her eyes fastened on the lawyer while Billy dealt the cards. Billy liked Glonell and Glonell liked Billy. But all her attention was fastened on the lawyer as though her eyes were a high-powered telescope fixed on a heavenly star. I felt a stab of jealousy; Glonell seemed to prefer the lawyer —whom she knew hardly at all, to me, who had known her all her life.

It was a moment of exquisite stillness; a leaf turning a circle in the silent current of a stream or a moment of sharp betrayal, I could not decide. Then that crazy little Glonell shot a left hook to my right jaw and all without ever moving her eyes off the lawyer. It came out of nowhere, as most things of a sudden and extraordinary nature, quite often do.

The lawyer, gasped.

I saw the Milky Way.

Billy's own jaw dropped. *Youuuuu little monkeeeee youuuuuuuu*, he said to Glonell.

Oh but she LOVED that. Her whole face tilted, a great wheel, on the anatomical angle of misery, spittle draped from her mouth to the top of her bright pink shirt collar.

I wanted to retaliate. I wanted immediate retribution for the hurt and humiliation she wrought. But I could not bring myself to retaliate. Besides, Billy got hold of my fist.

'Don't do it, Alice,' he said. 'Just don't.'

CANTON STREET

During the first week of March 1970 we were told to keep the back door locked. Everybody on Canton Street began locking their doors and windows where they hadn't before because they said, 'Times are different now.' Of course Glonell continued to leave our back door as wide open as the mouth of Moby Dick.

The big shift in home security first occurred with one of our sixteen-year-old neighbours who opened the door to a bear of a man. He had on a boiler suit and he carried a toolbox like he was a tradesman except he wasn't a tradesman but a psychopath pretending to be an air-conditioning repairman. The poor girl kind of blew away, a dried-up spider and her heartbroken parents moved to a state with gun laws so liberal they gave them away as a gift just for opening a bank account.

The world stopped when the Laceys got burgled. The Lacey sisters lived up the street. Mae, Millie, and Maxine, three blonde, blue-eyed girls, each two years apart and the oldest one, Mae – my good friend – was practising her scales on the piano when thieves carried off their colour television. They came through the back door while she banged away and never heard a thing until she went to turn on the TV and it was gone.

Opal Pike had no patience for salesmen. 'Nobody purchasing steak knives, magazine subscriptions, Burpee seeds, vacuum cleaner parts, a set of encyclopedias, snake oil, the weathervane don't need straightening, we don't need a lightning rod, and we still have a box of Girl Scout Cookies.'

'I ain't got none of those items, fine as they might be,' said the man she was addressing. He stood at the screen door holding a thick black book to his chest.

'I am not in the knife-selling business nor even remotely involved with sharp *objets d'art*,' he said.

He was slim in girth, wide in eye, and strong in tooth. Not cleanshaven, he had a pointy grey beard and moustache and a pocket watch attached to a chain looped through his front belt buckle. On his left pinky finger he wore a silver ring with a ruby stone. He wore a white suit and saddle shoes.

He removed a Confederate general's hat with a broad brim. His gray hair was thin and plastered back with perspiration. He referred to himself as a *divine representative of the Lord*... 'However employed terrestrially by The Sunshine Bible Company of Omaha, Nebraska,' then he inclined his head toward the screen door, in a little bow, like Opal was the Queen of England.

'Perhaps I can innerest you in a first-edition copy of the New Testament? Hand-bound from a group of Israelites who make them in the desert over yonder,' he pointed behind his head in the direction of the Stanley's house.

'Hmph,' said Opal Pike. She had her hand on her hip. She frowned at the man.

'Well, then how 'bout as a gift for that someone special? What about yer hubby? I am sure someone as lovely as yo'self must be accounted for.'

'He's dead,' said Opal.

'Why all the more reason then!' said the man. 'The holy book is a fine companion. It's like having God sittin' in a chair in yer livin' room havin' a chat.' Then he removed his hat and said, 'Oh – and I am truly sorry for your loss ma'am.'

'You don't have to waste your crowing ways on me – now you get going.' Opal was about to shut the interior door in his face – when the man said, '*Excusee-moy* but is that delicate and distinctly *au trez fee-mine* scent your toilette, ma'am?' he asked. He sniffed at the air for good measure.

Opal Pike was not used to a white man calling her 'ma'am' and she stopped just short of the door slam.

'Ma'am, if I may be so forthwith, might I inquire as to your vocational?'

'Sanitation,' said Opal.

'Have you been to Lesotho?' he asked.

'Why, no,' she said.

'Nor I,' said the man with a sigh. He took off his hat. He wiped his forehead with a filthy hanky he removed with a flourish from the breast pocket of his long ragged grey wool coat with two rows of brass buttons. 'I do plan to go and help the dear little children there, one day,' he said.

Opal thought, What's one bible? Her niece, a stripper at the Pink Pussy on 3rd Street, might find some redemption in its words.

'How much you asking for one?'

'It's regular $2.25 but I am amiable to accept two dollar and twenty cents,' the man scraped and bowed.

Opal went off to get her little eel skin purse. In the interim he pressed his face tight up against the screen door and with one roving dark eye he saw fine oriental rugs and oil paintings of Paris and another one of sailboats in a harbor; a sterling silver champagne bucket and then his gaze stopped at a curious creature with spittal hanging like dainty lace all from the fine curve of a child's mouth staring back at him.

'Well, hello,' said the man.

She was breathing heavily. The hot weather bothered her, made her heart work harder.

'That fine lady is gonna buy a Bible from me.'

Glonell stared.

'Ain't you all sugary looking?' said the man.

Glonell stared.

'What's yer name?'

Glonell stared.

'Cat got yer tongue?'

Glonell stared.

'Is that goddess your mama? 'Cause I hear you ain't got a daddy no more on this earthly plane.' The man pretended to wipe away tears; he made his face long and his mouth droop.

Glonell stared.

'That's a mighty fine vehicle out there,' he said, referring to the gold Cadillac parked in front of the house.

'That's my daddy's,' croaked Glonell.

'Is that so?' said the man. 'An I s'pose you is old enough to drive it, are you?'

'Yeah,' said Glonell.

'Well, now,' said the man, 'I see the cat gave yer tongue back.'

Opal returned with the money.

'Amen,' said the man. 'Praise, Jesus.'

Opal let the screen door open just wide enough to hand him the money and snatch the bible; he slid a foot inside held firm against the door jamb.

'It's going to be a regular scorcher today I reckon,' said the man.

'Over 90 degrees,' she said.

'Already feels like 199,' said the man waving his hat across his face like a fancy Chinese fan.

'Might I trouble you for a glass o' water? I am feeling a bit parched in the brutality of the glare.'

Opal didn't budge.

'It would be mighty Christian of you,' said the man. 'I'd be much obliged, ma'am.'

'You wait here,' she said, indicating with her hand to get his foot out of her screen door so she could shut it. 'You lettin'

the flies in.' And for a split second the man's face twisted up –
a dark storm travelling fast but Opal Pike didn't take notice –
she had turned in the direction of the kitchen. However
Glonell kept staring.

'I'll bet someone sweet as you likes candy,' he cooed.

Glonell didn't answer she just stood there breathing dragon-
like.

'You like sourballs? I got some lemon ones right here in
my pocket.'

'I like Sugar Babies,' her voice was hoary and gravelled, old
for a child.

'I'm fresh outta those,' said the man. 'But I tell you what,
next time I'm in the neighbourhood I'm gonna come back
with a pack of Sugar Babies just for you.'

Glonell smiled. She really did like Sugar Babies. And the
man smiled back because he thought: 'Ask and the door shall
be opened.'

FIREWATER

I don't know what my brother saw when his eyes were closed. I can't even say what he saw in reality when they were open. But something had happened to him when he'd gone fishing. He'd gone to the river one way and he came back another. He turned as fast as a leaf in a storm. He spoke in fervent whispers to Juan Goldstein. They were like Indian braves from the same crazy tribe of which I was not a member.

Yet when did I first hear about the Indian? Who Billy said was a big man. Not in height so much as vision. He could see things, like spacemen in silver suits walking off with a farmer's cattle, like possibilities. Anybody can see possibilities. They don't cost a dime.

Joseph Lightfoot stood six-foot three inches tall. His black hair fell rain-like around his strong jaw and ran down his back like a herd of buffalo. He wore an old army coat with brass buttons and a slouch black hat with a flat brim. His nose had been broken five times but his teeth were straight. His dark eyes glittered. He would describe himself as detached but not indifferent. And he'd say, 'I don't like bowling. I'm a billiards man, myself.'

Joseph Lightfoot joined the Marines and got shipped off to Vietnam. 'I didn't join actually, they drafted me. It was going alright until you had to shoot someone you didn't know. It didn't work out with the Marines,' he said.

When he got back Joseph Lightfoot was twenty-five years old and he walked to New Jersey. He took some seasonal fruit-picking work on a peach farm. At night he slept under the fantastic and complex stars in fields of tall grass and wheat running alongside the highway. When he got sick of peaches, he walked over to Delaware to pick tomatoes.

'The things I have seen,' he'd say to Billy. Then he'd make

52

up all sorts of bullshit about ancient giants staring down the holes of wigwams.

In the winter Joseph Lightfoot spent a lot of time at the pool hall. He drank alcohol boiled up with pot leaves he called 'Firewater'.

'Where do you concoct this stuff?' he was asked.

'In a bathtub,' he said.

Now and then the alcohol backfired, and one of his customers, mostly individuals on welfare or parole, would go blind and threaten to kill the Indian. Then they'd get their sight back and buy some more.

When he wasn't playing pool or picking fruit, he occupied one of the condemned buildings near the pool hall. In the wintertime he walked to the river. He'd strip down naked, and swim in the freezing waters. 'Like my father did, and his father, and his father, before him,' he'd say.

Joseph Lightfoot liked to fish the river for brook trout. He cooked it up on an old Coleman's stove. He'd eat the fish with sweetcorn from a can, sometimes pumpkin. He used a slingshot in the woods on small wild turkey. When he'd had enough, he'd just go to the supermarket and buy a sirloin steak. This is where he bumped into the rich widow. She was forty-five, attractive, and her dead husband had owned a lot of used car lots.

The rich widow took an oddball kind of fancy to the Indian. His ebony eyes flowed through her, two waterfalls of light. She thought about the images of dead Americans hanging in the local museum. People called Bull Bear, Black Kettle, and One-Eye. 'Any relation?' she asked.

'Not a one,' he said.

The girls his age didn't stick around for very long. As far as they were concerned, Joseph Lightfoot was never going to make a decent living and women need that, a decent living and all.

However the rich widow felt the American Indian gave her a push in a direction less singular than her dead husband, whom if she had to confess had become, in the end, a great porker of a man and as flaccid in the penile department as a dead rattler. Things were going pretty good at the rich widow's house; all he had to do was satisfy her strong sexual nature.

During the freezing winter months she brought Joseph Lightfoot to Palm Beach, Florida, where many rich widows keep a second home. Beneath a flaming purple sky at twilight, Joseph Lightfoot would poke her up her rich widow's Pocahontas while she whooped like a crane. He quite enjoyed the sunset.

It was a pretty good arrangement all around: he'd fuck her and drink all her spirits and beer. Then one afternoon the rich widow came home from a bridge game to find Joseph Lightfoot had stolen a flamingo from the national park.

'It used to be our land,' he said.

But this did not impress her. Certainly not in the same way the flamingo now cooking on her outdoor BBQ did. Joseph Lightfoot turned it with a pair of tongs. Its pink head and long legs scattered through the buffalo grass of the rich widow's backyard.

The widow was horrified. Then she kicked out the Indian. He caught a bus up North, one-way ticket on the Greyhound, and he slept most of the two-day journey while thinking up a new plan: a power hose business to wash down cement driveways.

'Where's the Indian?' I asked my brother.

'Downtown.'

'Downtown, where?'

'He shoots pool. Go see for yourself.'

I would have liked to go. I surely would, but not there. The pool hall was in a neighbourhood of three-storey narrow red-brick dwellings with CONDEMNED signs nailed to their boarded-up doors.

The windows were broken and birds had come to build their nests inside. I was sure people still lived there and I could feel the cold on their faces in the winter, and the heat of the long humid summer. I couldn't see them, but they could see us – and with clarity, too, within the confines of their darkened space.

MARIANNE MOORE

Billy said the Indian had moved from downtown to live in an abandoned yellow school bus. It was a beat-up school bus with the seats torn out. It was dumped in the woods where Joseph Lightfoot's ancestors used to stamp out trails, where they used bird's claws for fish hooks, where they all lived in the Big House, not far from the old Indian School, where Billy would sell cars one day and where the poet Marianne Moore used to live. She wrote poems with titles like: 'Nine Tangerines' and 'Those Various Scalpels'.

Joseph Lightfoot did not read Marianne Moore but he did grow his own lettuce. The bus was concealed in the woods. He called it 'the Big House'.

When Billy and Juan weren't breaking into uninhabited and desolate property, they'd wander over to the Civil War battlefield due south. There they threw rocks at each other from opposite sides. Then they'd visit Joseph Lightfoot.

'He inhales turpentine,' said Billy.

'You think he's normal?' I said.

'Who is?' he said.

The Indian lived on 'The Wedge' that circle of land that did not quite meet the corner of a square.

Billy said he liked to sit on a folding beach chair in front of the old yellow school bus and drink beer. On freezing winter days Joseph Lightfoot spent afternoons in the library. 'It's heated,' he said, 'and free.' He spoke about the diorama at the library. The one with the wax Indian cooking fish on the open fire. He said he ate some mushrooms and nearly had heart failure when he saw the diorama Indian walking around on Union Street wearing a duffle coat. And a do-rag covering his dick.

Joseph Lightfoot asked, more to the God of nature and physical and mental laws invisible around him, what makes you think we wore pathetic shit like that?

'Because you did,' said Juan.

'Fuck me,' said the Indian. He threw his switchblade, bullseye at the trunk of the furthest great needle pine; it went slicing through the wood-sweet air until the hilt of the blade went thwack.

Then the Indian talked about the two souls: one in the heart and one in the blood. How the heart soul travelled after death but the blood soul walked around earth scaring the shit out of people and it's not that Billy and Juan were interested in a cultural debate but they quite enjoyed drinking his beer, smoking his dope, and listening to his point-of-view in general.

Of course Joseph Lightfoot mentioned something he saw through the crosshairs of his rifle – *takes a person's soul all the way to disbelief and back*. But he never said what it was. Instead he got up. Turned his back on them and walked through the woods, an Indian lost on a trail of dark feeling.

THE STANLEYS

When everybody's doors and windows were on lock-down that March, workmen arrived at the other end of Canton Street with diggers and cement. They worked through the spring and the hottest months, straight through a golden autumn and into the chilly early winter until they erected a home with a large pointed roof and great panes of glass. The house belonged to the Stanleys. The Stanleys were God's gift to enmity, not because they were destructive or bellicose; they were as exacting as a Native American's arrow. As soon as they moved in they planted a whole line of full-grown pine trees blocking a view of the mountains. They hired Joseph Lightfoot to hose down their circular drive.

The Stanley boy (Randolph) was two years younger than his sister, the Stanley girl (Stacy). The Stanleys were the sort of people who had commissioned an oil painting of their dog.

Billy and I hated their dog. We used to throw crab apples at it.

The Stanley boy had a moustache at eight years old. The Stanley girl spoke with a whine; her voice on the perpetual edge of hysteria. The Stanley children's clothes came from Saks Fifth Avenue. Ours came from Sears. The Stanleys went to the opera and the theatre. Billy and I hung around the local cemetery. The Stanley children read *Little Women* and *Billy Budd*. We read comic books.

The Stanley children hated and dreaded us. But we only hated them. Sometimes, when I had nothing to do, I'd meander down the other end of Canton Street and pick the flowers off the Stanleys' magnolia tree.

One time I'd been so busy plucking away I hadn't heard Mrs Stanley sneak up on me like some bizarre suburban tarantula. Her hair was wild, ghost-white and tangled. In contrast, her black eyes sunken and she had long eye teeth. She wore a white cotton dressing gown; it could have been an apparition: but it was outside, 8am and talking, so I knew it was just Mrs Stanley.

'Hello, Alice Sycamore,' Mrs Stanley whispered in my ear.

I nearly jumped twenty feet. And that was all she said: *Helloooooo, Alice Sycamore...*

Trying to rise above the awkwardness into which I had now been thrust I said, 'Hello, Mrs Stanley.'

Silence.

I would rather Mrs Stanley said something more diffuse and less roundabout than nothing, while I stood there with half her tree in my hands.

The bright sun washed away all of Mrs Stanley's features. A blank wall I wanted to spray paint.

'Say hi to Stacey,' I smiled.

Not a word.

A car rumbled down Canton Street. A dog barked at another dog somewhere. A plane flew overhead coming or going – and not caught red-handed taking the Stanleys' plant-life before I wasn't sure if I should offer to put the magnolias back onto the limb with some glue or offer a half-assed apology. I couldn't make up my mind. Then I decided.

'Well, it was real nice chatting with you, Mrs Stanley.'

But she remained tight-lipped, corpse-like.

'I'll just return these...' I pushed all the flowers into the crook of her folded arms and ran.

Not long after, Billy and Juan put a dead snake on the Stanleys' driveway. Mrs Stanley spotted them from her kitchen window and just about had kittens. She walked all the way down Canton Street until she reached our house, carrying the snakeskin straight out in front of her on the end of BBQ tongs.

'Why would you put this *thing* on my driveway?' she demanded.

'Ah,' said Juan, 'Thank you. We've been looking for that.'

One day the Stanley girl and I will live five blocks from each other in a great east-coast city. We will see each other at the fruit seller, at the newspaper kiosk, on the downtown express train. I will pretend not to see her. She lives in a three-bedroom penthouse condominium her daddy bought for her while I share an apartment with a drunk from Detroit.

'Alice?' she will say. 'My *God* – is that *you*?'

'Hey,' I will say.

She will ask me if I want to have lunch. I don't. I meet her.

'How's Minky?' I ask about the Stanleys' dog.

'Oh, Alice,' she says, as though I have just poured ketchup over my head. 'She died twelve years ago.'

'Sorry,' I say.

'You and your brother were mean to her.'

'Hmmm,' I say. 'We were.'

'I heard about Billy,' she said.

Silence: Terrible, lengthy and complex. The Stanley girl becomes a whiskery rat, pink-eyed, long-ringed grey tail she's biting the fleas off with big buck teeth. I tap the tabletop. It is black and reflective. I can see all the way to retrospective hell and back. Something had happened to Billy that March afternoon when he went down to the river to go fishing. He'd gone one way but came back another. Like one of the magnolia buds Mrs Stanley made me, in the end, try to re-root.

And for a moment I think about the river: the colour, the flow, the light, and shadow.

And about the Stanley girl, who still whines when she talks.

And about Billy... then I try not to think about any of it, at all.

THE GENERAL

When Billy was twelve years old he met a stranger by the river. On a pleasant and windless March afternoon in 1970. The sun cast a net of hazy light across the earth and the face of the fast-flowing water. Years later Billy would tell me the man looked like a Civil War general.

'Like the beard and brass buttons?' I asked.

'Yeah, all that,' he said.

He didn't carry a sword and scabbard just an old Pepsi cup. He was asking Billy to fill the cup for him. From Billy's canteen, if Billy didn't mind and all, he'd drank his up and he was thirsty. The man removed his officer's hat. It had initials above the brim: C.S.A. but where fancy gold cord should have been wound, only a piece of twine encircled the base and hung down, in two frayed knots. He removed the bashed-in hat now and fanned himself.

The air around them smelled of sweet pine sap and decaying leaves. Fishing for brown speckled trout Billy had had some luck already. The man stooped to admire two fat trout swimming in a tin bucket Billy kept beside him.

'Fine-looking fish. You've caught them yourself?' asked the man.

'Yep,' said Billy.

The man straightened up rubbing his hands together. Then he looked about him sharpish, like he was expecting somebody. When he didn't see anybody he coughed and spat. He wiped his brow with a paper napkin.

'A mighty pretty spot you're fishing at. I come up from Atlanta,' said the man. 'Been driving for two days straight.' He rubbed the back of his fleshy neck. He threw the used napkin into the river. The wind blew it straight back onto his saddle shoe.

Bracken and fern and large overflowing mulberry bushes, great birch and blue spruce grew wild behind them. It was a lonely spot. The water and the woods absorbed the sounds of the road beyond, swallowing the roar of large trucks passing.

'I can see the freight trains coming across the bridge from here,' said Billy, pointing into the distance ahead, into nothing.

'Boys like trains,' said the man, 'and fishing,' he leaned forward again, touching the trout in the bucket with two fingers.

'Whatchya call this river?' the man asked Billy.

'The Susquehanna River,' said Billy.

'Yes, I knowed it's that,' said the man, pronouncing it "SusqQUEEhanna." 'But it's an Injun name ain't it? Don't just mean what it sounds like… it means something else.'

Billy shrugged. He didn't know what it meant. Something tugged on his line. He leaned away; wound in his reel.

'Take the Calooshatachee,' said the man. 'It ain't a grand river, nor do it shine silver like a dime. But it means the same on both accounts.'

'What?' said Billy, only half-listening. Much like he did in Mrs Sprague's geography class when he didn't care about counting to twenty in German and she made him do calisthenics in the rain.

'Are you deaf?' asked the man.

Billy kept a firm eye on his fishing line being pulled downstream in the strong current.

'The word "Caloosahatchee" already means "river". If you say "Caloosahatchee River" you're just sayin' "river-river",' said the man. He spat out a piece of chewing gum. 'Which ain't too smart if you stop an' think on it.'

Billy didn't much care about the name of a river, 'I don't think a river cares what it's called, not like a person might care,' said Billy, who in later years knew a set of Chinese twins called Wing Wing and Ding Ding.

'Well I'm not saying a river can think about anything except goin' along with its own God-given momentum. I'm just pointing out a curiosity. Ain't you got curiosities?' asked the man. His eyes resting on Billy's back and shoulders.

Billy shrugged.

'Only the dead don't have curiosities,' said the man.

'I think the dead do,' Billy said.

The man shook his head. 'Now ain't you all clever.'

He kept up his chit-chat a little longer, the man. He thanked Billy for the water, he had a 'rendeevoos' he said, and had to 'skeedaddle'.

After the man departed Billy turned back to the river. The sun was changing from bright yellow to burnished gold. A cloud of mayflies skirted the edges of the shallows where they hoped not to be pulled down, drowned, and eaten by trout.

HOG-TIED

Billy reached down to pick up his bucket of fish. Water sloshed over the sides of the metal bucket and onto his bare feet, he walked into the river, up to his knees, and released the fish just below the water's surface, against the swift current, the fish refilling their circulatory systems, gills enlarged, eyes adjusting to the darkness pierced by shafts of waning light. The boy let them slip: shining, spotted, glittery-skinned.

Alone between a sinking sun and descending twilight he listened to the night insects beginning their hum and the distant sound of traffic beyond reach of the river and the woods.

However the sound of twigs cracking and dried leaves crunching beneath footfall gave Billy pause to look toward the woods behind him. He saw the flash of brass buttons, and the man shoving aside oak fern and woodland flax.

Billy glanced at the ground around him for a ring, a pocket watch, a billfold. Billy thought the man probably left something – or else he needed directions back to Georgia, which Billy couldn't help him with – he could only direct him as far south as the Lincoln Avenue Bridge which would take the man toward Gettysburg. But before Billy had a chance to speak the man loomed over him, talking fast, fly-blown and maggoty into Billy's ear. Everything slowed down around Billy. The insects' hum died out. The river got quiet and watchful. Even the wind seemed to come to a halt.

The tiniest of hairs on the back of the Billy's neck prickled. The man's saddle shoes were sinking halfway into the ochre-colour river sand. His eyes burned. He lightly brushed his outstretched palm against Billy's curly hair. His voice sounded harsh, agitated, thrilled.

'I meant to ask,' the man spoke. '*You* a mulatto – aintchya? 'cause they be hot blooded,' he said, running a tongue across his lips.

Billy's brow furrowed. His heart pounded in his chest loud as the train's whistle forging the cleft in the mountain. He could feel the vibration, hear the ringing, but whether it was his heart or the whistle, he wasn't sure.

'I seen me a mulatto in New Orleans doing his business with a hog. I paid good money to watch while the sow squeal like a ratty old whore.'

Billy tried to imagine what the man was describing. 'They're intelligent, you know. Did you know a pig's got a particular mental capacity?' the man asked Billy.

Billy was too petrified to reply. Besides, he didn't know anything about a pig's IQ.

The blood in Billy's veins and arteries froze up when he figured he was about to be hog-tied and poked up the backside by a man who looked like a Confederate general from the American Civil War.

'Get up,' said the man.

Billy didn't move. Half-seated on a river rock during the exchange, his eyes skimmed the surface of the river for tiny bubbles of air breaking the pattern of flowing water. The man whirled behind Billy then shoved a knee into Billy's lower back.

'I told you boy, get up. Now let's go.'

By the time Billy could properly hold a fork he could hold a fishing rod. The first one, an antique cane rod, came from our Welsh great grandfather but Billy wasn't holding a fishing rod now. Instead he was sitting on a rock. The rock had not settled into the silt of the river so long that it could only be extracted by a pickaxe or a crowbar. Billy leapt up and struck the pervert in the head with it.

The man stumbled backwards, falling into the river. Into the swift-flowing waters swollen from snow-melt, and heavy spring rains.

SITUATION ETHICS

He grabbed his fishing rod and tried to shut his tackle box. He was not in a good frame of mind having whacked a stranger in the head with a rock.

Billy touched the spot on his back where the man had shoved his knee. It made Billy's own knees tremble, made his hands shake. Meanwhile, the general had managed to crawl out of the river downstream and onto the shore. He had twigs in his beard and his eyes leaked river water. 'I'm gonna kill that boy,' the man spat out some river weed. 'I'm gonna teach him a lesson but good and righteous,' the man shouted, punching the air with his fist.

Billy flew through the thicket, pounding the leaf-strewn trail, leaping over thick tree roots. He was going to make it out to Union Street where he knew he'd be safe then he tripped over the rotting trunk of a Sugar Maple.

Billy fell flat on his back. He felt his lungs collapse, his kidneys bruise. His fishing rod jumped out of his hand and his tackle box caught the side of his face, a sharp-edge cut below his right eye. Blood trickled down, a tributary merging with the ocean of his mouth. He wasn't sure if he'd broken a bone, snapped his spine. The March chill trapped in the winter earth crept quickly through his thin jacket and jeans. He saw the canopy of trees above him, mostly bare branches, the buds and new leaves just beginning to form but he couldn't really see them. The back of his skull had taken a whack, his vision blurred. But his hearing was intact. He strained hard to listen: the footfall – twigs, branches, cracking – *somebody's coming*. If Billy remained still maybe he would melt away, like so many atoms dissolving. He could barely breathe; he didn't dare move a finger. But his heart was hammering wildly and without precedent when the trees overhead suddenly disappeared; replaced by a shadow cast across the boy, a violent storm gathering. There was someone peering at him too, bent over the old mossy-and-decayed remains of the oak.

'Say, son, I wasn't gonna hurt you for real; you know that? Don't you, boy?'

The man talked, loosening his belt and unzipping his fly. He also managed to pin one of Billy's arms down with his shoe. 'I just wanna us ta' be friends,' said the man. 'And by the way, you ain't bein' too friendly – but don't worry, we gonna fix all that.'

Billy thought he must be dreaming. This situation was happening to somebody else and he was watching them on television. He really wanted to be watching television.

'You got such fine woolly hair,' he said. 'Pretty for a boy.'

Billy remained silent while the man made all sorts of proclamations, pantings and mewlings.

He wiped away a blood drop on the boy's face with his pinky finger. Then he stuck the finger in his mouth and sucked it clean. The taste of Billy's blood appeared to excite the man. His nostrils flared and his lips quivered. He wiped blood leaking from the gash in his own head and forced several bloody fingers into Billy's horrified mouth.

'Now we *is* best friends,' said the man.

The man's blood tasted iron and foul. Billy gagged then spat it back in his face.

The man laughed. 'Now that ain't no way to treat a friend,' he said whacking the heel of his saddle shoe into Billy's arm. Billy thought he'd broken it; he heard a snap, felt a burst of pain – but it was just the man dropping onto a pile of dried leaf and branch, onto his knees.

'First I's gonna whomp you like I do my best hog and if

you don't play nice I is gonna wring yer neck like I do my scrawniest chicken and let the buzzards pick out your eyeballs – 'cause that's the first thing them ugly birds eat, is the eyeballs – did you know'd that?'

Billy did not know that.

'I was just talking about curiosities. You *got* to have curiosities.' The man kicked Billy in his side at the same time as pushing him onto his stomach. This change offered Billy site of an object resting by a half-buried car tyre six feet away. It just so happened to belong to Billy too, the possession – a birthday gift from our uncle with the metal plate in his head, for Billy's twelfth birthday. It had flown out of Billy's jacket pocket when he tripped. The man didn't notice it because the man was too full of pervert jumpiness and thrill.

'Now we kin do this the easy way, or we can do it hard,' said the man. He took a handful of Billy's hair and yanked him up.

'Easy or hard?' sneered the man. Then he patted his pants pocket, 'cause I got Missy here – know who she be?'

Billy paused. He wasn't sure if the man called his penis 'Missy'.

'"Missy" be my trusty bow knife. She better than a wife. But not as good as a sweet honey of a mistress. And certainly she don't come nowhere near to a fresh boy like you. Now I have had about enough of this shit – you gonna make this worth my whole while – get on all fours.' The man kicked Billy a few more times in his ribs for good, pervert, measure. His knee pressed hard against Billy's lower back.

'Ready or not, boy,' the man whispered into Billy's ear – 'my humdinger be thick as a ham and ready to poke right up yer Yankee tail.' The man let out a horrible grunt like a hog before lowering himself down.

Fear and adrenalin, being as good as a poke in the eye

helped Billy knock the old pervert sideways then he did a baseball-style slide to the tyre like it was home plate.

He was not expecting to be challenged by the boy who only seconds before acted more like a dead fish and who now aimed a mini Colt .45 straight at the general's dick.

'Jesus Mary and Joseph, son – you put that gun down before somebody gits in a whole lotta shit – d'ya innerstan what I'm tryin' to convey?' The last thing he expected was a kid with a handgun aimed at his dick. The man tried to do up his zipper.

Billy slowly got up. The gun going point-blank with him, while the man dropped to his own knees hoping it wasn't obvious to the boy he'd started pissing in his pants because the gun kind of evened everything up. 'Hey, I've got some candy. You like candy?' The man dug into his pockets. 'Here – here, you kin have it all,' he said. He threw half a roll of cherry flavoured Lifesavers on the ground and a couple of lemon sourballs. The lemon ones struck the top of Billy's sneaker.

'Go on,' said the man, indicating with a flick of his hand – 'take them – it's all I got – I don't have no money.'

Billy stepped on the sourball until it crunched into the earth.

But being a wily pervert, and used to such means and ways, the man sensed Billy's momentary uncertainty. 'I guess you gonna just have to shoot me,' said the man.

Billy said nothing. He took off the safety catch.

The pervert threw his hands in the air. 'An' you kill me, you goin' to the 'lectric chair.'

The electric chair occupied an anxious place in Billy's imagination. The wily old pervert sniffed out the hesitation… 'I knowed people been put to death in the chair. Thirty-foot flames come jumping outta a man's skull like dancing demons. He don't just get 'lectrocuted but gets set on fire. You kill me you gonna burn fer sure up and die like a boiled pig's belly.'

'No,' said Billy, 'that won't happen.'

'And why is that?'

''Cause I'm just a kid.'

Billy fired a single shot in the sky above him. The black birds shrieked and beat their wings, lifting them into flight, sudden and frenzied.

The man followed the birds. He flapped his arms with a whoop-whoop, zigzagging inbetween the trees with Billy in pursuit firing shots; some hit the trunks ricocheting and pockmarking the earth as the man staggered toward the river landing face-first into the brackish water, a thick crimson-coloured streak trailing along in the current carrying him swiftly downstream.

THE ROOT LADY

There are just so many people you can trust in your life. In Billy's case he had Juan Goldstein, as reliable as the chemical make-up of salt, and by mid-afternoon the following day, Billy decided to go back to look for the man. He tried to convince Juan to go along however Juan needed no convincing. 'You think you shot him?' asked Juan.

'I think I did,' said Billy, 'And a couple of pine trees.'

Back then, on a regular day, Billy and Juan stood silent and watchful on the roof of Juan's parents' red-brick colonial house in the middle of dark freezing winter nights looking for astronomical anomalies in the sky. During the day they waited for deer to emerge, bloated and empty-eyed, tossed out of the weir in the river. The weir pulled helpless creatures trapped on ice floes or fallen tree trunks straight into the jaws of a crushing mechanical wave. It tumbled them over and over until their lungs filled with river water and their souls got spat out the other side, to continue their journey anyway, downstream and out to sea.

Sometimes they took a canoe from The Indian Trading Post. They'd hoist it above their shoulders and drop it over their heads trudging through the woods to the river's edge, to go fishing all day and return the boat after dark.

The Indian Trading Post rented out those canoes, antiquated, painted gunmetal; with wooden seams that gave a person splinters. They were stacked like a pyramid of silver fishes behind the store.

The Indian Trading Post advertised genuine Amish quilts for sale. The quilts were pegged to a sagging old wash line; the patchwork pieces fading in the strong summer light or else getting rained or snowed on. Tourists stopped and bought them. The quilts were cobbled together from old underwear, undershirts, and tracksuit bottoms by a woman about as Amish as a blue-footed duck. However Mona (half-Nanticoke, half-Irish) was adept at curing a variety of human ailments using rattlesnake innards and indigenous weeds. 'You gotta chop the head off the snake good and clean. Then soak its heart 'till it double in size.'

'What's that a cure for?' Billy asked her.

'Athlete's foot,' she said and spat on the ground. 'Care for some fudge?' (The shop also sold peanut brittle and saltwater taffy.)

'Can we borrow a canoe?' asked Juan seeing as she was sitting on a tree stump next to them that particular day.

'Normally you just take one – why you askin' for a change?'

'Because you're sitting beside them,' said Juan.

Mona sat on a stump from a White Oak tree, burlap sacking filled with oily rags and clothing at her feet. She leaned on a crooked stick of witch hazel. She used it to find underground veins of water. 'Why don't you just get water from the tap?' Juan asked her.

'Ain't the same.' She reached into her long jet-black hair wound into a loose and sloppy bun at the top of her skull. Stuck through like an Indian's arrow was a half-smoked cigar. She pulled it out, lit it with a wooden match she struck against the side of her well-calloused bare foot and puffed hard. Then she adjusted her big, square eyeglasses to look more closely at Billy.

'I saw you fishing just before the blue moon,' Mona said to Billy.

Billy said nothing.

She stared at Billy. Billy stared back.

'How's Miss Opal?'

'Alright I guess,' he said.

'You tell her Mona be askin' for her.'

Billy nodded. Jaw tight.

'You look like you been through the wars, boy.' She pointed to the cut under Billy's eye, to the purple bruises and long scrapes on his neck and arms.

'I tripped,' said Billy.

'Is that so?' said Mona. ''Cause I seen a man go into the woods but he don't come out – you know? Then I seen you about half hour later running up toward the road like a demon grabbed on to yer behind – you know what I is referrin' to?' Mona fastened her snake eyes on Billy. 'Dressed like a Confederate.' Mona spat. She didn't like Confederates.

'You kin get the electric chair like Lew's cousin Dermit.'

'Do they still electrocute people in this state?' asked Juan.

Mona counted on her fingers. 'Eight years ago Dermit got fried. The flames shooting straight out the top of his head, like it was July 4th in there.'

Billy's heart pounded so hard in his chest he was certain the old witch could see. Before he could refute anything Mona cut him off: 'You bring me back some yellow root and jimson an' I won't say nothin' 'bout the boat you was fixin' to steal.'

'Borrow,' said Juan. 'Only borrow.'

Carrying the canoe over their heads Mona's words trailed behind, an ice pick striking at the heart of Billy's culpability: 'Bring me my roots, Billy Sycamore, and I won't say nothin' to no one what I think you done.'

THE BOY SCOUTS OF AMERICA

The river ran high and mighty and didn't stop to wait or think about what two boys were doing paddling fast towards the Lincoln Avenue Bridge looking for a dead man. The river, of course, doesn't think about anything but itself. But that's the ways and means of the river. Whatever got trapped or was meant to be in the river and swept up in the current was all subject to the time and motion of the moment.

They discussed the situation as if they were talking about the outcome of a baseball game.

They did this while paddling Mona's canoe to an island mid-river, a migratory bird home for the Common Loon, Lesser Scaup, and Bufflehead.

'Let's just get onto Hawk Island,' said Billy.

The canoe cut through the grey water below Hawk Island where Joseph Lightfoot's ancestors hung around catching fish eight thousand years ago.

'My people were song and dance people,' said Joseph Lightfoot.

They also formed part of the material used to construct a canal on the river. Hundreds of cartloads of Indian bones were found in a burial mound by workers digging the canal. They mixed the bones with concrete.

The sun ducked behind a cloud. They rounded the eastern tip of the island, jumped out and pulled the canoe onto the mud-flat shoreline. The ground beyond was awash in brown and yellow leaves. The deciduous forest of river birch, sycamore, and silver maple grew fantastic and green overhead. Underneath they walked over blue-eyed grass, umbrella magnolia, and flat-leaved pondweed growing in tangles, hedges, and mounds.

It's difficult to say what Billy expected to find. They trudged around the periphery of the island looking for a sign of a Confederate general cooking beans on an open fire, alive if not pissed off as all kingdom come having been outwitted by a twelve-and-a-half year old and Billy wouldn't be a murderer and face life in prison, or worse – the electric chair. Instead they bumped into The Boy Scouts of America.

The Scout Leader was dressed like a giant child in green khaki shorts and yellow kerchief and a brown felt hat pinched in at both sides. He seemed the sort of person who would vote for Ralph Nader in a presidential election. He felt if it wasn't for Ralph Nader, America would not have anti-lock brakes, airbags, rack and pinion steering. He believed things like independent suspension made America great. That's what he told the troop of boy scouts gathered around him: 'Independent suspension changed *everything*. And underground parking garages.' He practically had tears in his eyes, the Scout Leader.

All this time, Billy and Juan kept a low profile behind a crumbling stone wall a farmer built during the Civil War. They spied on the Boy Scouts of America. They did not wish to participate in the scouting community. But the Scout Leader, who had X-ray scout's vision, spotted Billy and Juan trying to sneak off. They looked about as scout-worthy to him as two airplane hijackers. The Scout Leader thought, 'Look at those two weasely little shits.'

The Boy Scouts of America is for fine American boys who don't go diving into beanbag chairs at Woolworths and go crashing into the glass aquariums causing three thousand dollars' worth of damage (Juan) or shoot a bible salesman in the head (Billy). His whole expression said: 'you two are nothing but degenerates – now get your honky afro (Billy) and your hippie-beaded (Juan) asses off this island before I beat the living crap out of you with a belt like I do my own kids.'

Of course the Scout Leader thought this but he wouldn't dare say it. He had an example to set.

'Say, fellas,' he waved to Billy and Juan. 'We're just about to have a talk on Bush Etiquette – how'd you like to join in?'

Juan looked around. Billy said, 'Yes, sir,' and they both saluted.

'What little assholes,' thought the Scout Leader.

The Scout Leader cleared his throat. 'If you have to shit in the woods you put the paper in the brown paper bag and bring it home with you to dispose of in a proper container or facility. You don't let the paper blow away with the wind. If you don't have any paper use grass or leaves – *capiche*?'

'Now some of you might notice various-sized piles of excretion. Make no doubt about it this is from the animal population. And although excretions are often seen on the top of rocks, we should not try to emulate this. So please, please, *please* do your business off the trail. For the big jobbies you'll need to have a spade to dig a hole and cover it over with dirt and twigs… and make sure your business is at least 150 feet from the nearest water source. Nobody wants to pan for your gold.'

The Boy Scouts of America weren't smiling. Not one of them chuckled or snickered or guffawed. They looked as serious as if the Scout Leader talked about how to bury a grandmother.

The Scout Leader removed his bright yellow Boy Scout of America regulation kerchief around his neck. He blew his nose in it and retied it. 'Any questions?' The Boy Scouts of America had no questions. They unequivocally accepted the method and practices for burying their own shit in the woods.

Juan raised his hand. 'Sir – can you apply the same principals to the burial of anything made out of carbon?'

The Scout Leader removed his brown felt hat and scratched his head, as if he hadn't thought about anything made out of carbon ever before.

THROWING BEER CANS AT THE LOCAL WILDLIFE

Billy began staying out longer and coming home later.

This was also when Billy talked about the Nazi by the river. He'd tell all of this stuff to Opal Pike and me, and we'd listen to him until Opal would say: 'For sure you making this up.' Billy said the Nazi owned a Christmas tree farm. He said the trees were being grown in a swastika pattern on the Nazi's property.

Billy loved Opal because he was used to her ways. When people get used to somebody's ways the heart and the mind can rest quiet. But when distrust pours like concrete the river doesn't flow right and there were still plenty of blank spaces, not least in our father's head rattling around like so many question marks regarding his antics at the Bluebird Motel. Opal Pike liked to remind him, particularly while clutching a straw broom in the left fist of her oversized hand he best confess his tribulations or he *goin' to burn in the fires of Hell.* 'Ain't no good gonna come of a cheater – you bringing doom on this whole family.' But our father appeared to have no idea what she was talking about – and even if he did he pretended not to. He'd remind her he wasn't a Christian and ask her to please not stand in front of the TV.

One afternoon Billy saw a bear in the woods. This was when the river flowed shallow and lazy and Billy meandered around the Susquehanna River Valley opening his spirit to the mountain man bursting within him.

'What you do when you seen it?' Opal asked.

'Threw a beer can at it,' he said.

'You weren't afraid it was gonna come after you?'

'No,' he said, 'I put a lit firecracker in first, then threw it.'

Opal said Billy best be careful if he didn't want the Devil of mischief, the Devil of lies, the Devil as a total, all-enveloping entity to spit him out like a watermelon seed. 'An you didn't see no bear,' she spat back, 'and there ain't no Nazis, neither.' Of course a week later a hiker got mauled to death. And it was just common knowledge Mrs Sprague owned a set of Adolph Hitler's lobster forks.

I didn't think one way or another about Billy because he still seemed alright and besides I had my own life: running around with the Lacey sisters; smoking cigarettes with Tawny Milford because the Lacey sisters didn't smoke; making out with Todd Wertz behind the 7-11 on Tyler Avenue; flunking eight grade algebra – yes, I kept constructively busy for a nearly twelve year old – even taking Mrs Sprague on by insisting Billy and I *were* siblings – that she should check the school records to see we lived at the *same* address; or call our house: 232 1559 – but don't ask our father, I explained, 'because lately he answers the phone: *Sears and Roebuck.*' And the very fact I had the 'audacity' as she put it to 'tell her how to do her job' found me doing forty squat thrusts that autumn in the late November rain.

By Easter, Billy's subtly shifting demeanour: a sullen darkness suddenly shutting down his conversation when quite animated only a moment earlier; or a dead-eyed and monotonous mumbling about something he lost but needed to find began to quietly assert itself. He'd stare into space like he could see things invisible to the rest of us. Or he'd say: 'Did you see *that*?'

'See what?'

'George Washington…' he'd point to the set of beige drapes.

I'd look at the beige drapes in the lounge and see beige drapes.

Our father, given his own predicament would have thought it normal if Billy claimed to be George R. Custer; while our mother merely distilled it down to sulky adolescence. I finally started to pay more attention to my brother's mental state, and not just because Billy started seeing people in the soft furnishings; but it's impossible to ignore somebody who's started eating macaroni and cheese with their hands.

THE OLD METAL BRIDGE

When things don't act right people get interested. That's what Opal Pike used to say. In some places people can see a whale swim the wrong way up a river. Apparently a lot of people came out to watch. They are watching because the whale isn't acting right.

It was first spotted by a man on a bridge. He was crossing the bridge stretching across the river like slow-moving marble. The man thought he was seeing things. That's what the man told the newspapers, he said, 'I thought I was hallucinating.'

Billy used to hallucinate.

'What have you seen now?' I asked him.

'A Confederate general in the abandoned old house by the creek.'

'You're kidding – right?'

'He eats bean soup out of a can and he knows where we live.'

Billy reminded me of the ebb and flow of river water. He reminded me of the man on the bridge. He reminded me of the boys along the Susquehanna River holding a handgun to the head of a sculpture in the park. He reminded me of the sculpture. The clear winter light, the old metal bridge.

Opal Pike used to look at Billy and me and say things we couldn't understand. It wasn't obscure but straightforward pity which we couldn't grasp. 'You poor children,' she would say.

'Why, what's wrong with us?' asked Billy.

Maybe it was something she saw that we couldn't. But it wasn't for us to see yet; like a lot of thoughts and questions. It's hard to see sometimes.

Particularly when it's not yet safe to remember.

GRAVE ROBBERS

The flood waters had clawed at the earth with long wet river-fingers. It pulled elm and oak up by the tree roots. It gouged out the land like a terrible war and burst open caskets where bones had clinked around since the revolutionary war in America. The bones wore shredded filaments of red wool and pewter buttons. The coffins bobbed like so many strange boats. A grim curiosity, wind blowing through ribcages, rain pelting eye sockets, people woozy from the shock of all the loss and destruction found this rather witty, if not a pleasant downright distraction to cleaning up mud-drenched walls and floors. The general stood there, his officer's hat on his head; the drizzle falling around us, and he was thinking. 'I could see it in his whole manner, shark eyes following caskets, the buttons glint and lure – estimating,' said Billy – 'figuring how much he could get for the embellishments of the dead, antique and valuable, precious and extraordinary.' Billy pointed him out – and God knows I wanted to see the general for myself. The general seemed to worry Billy, as did the electric chair. I could not figure out who the general was, or what he had to do with my brother, or how death by electrocution and the general were inextricably bound, but by the following summer, when the river rose and flooded our town, Billy said the general was there. That he had come to observe the parade of the dead, in the local cemetery, like a thief.

'Look! There…!' he said.

But when I looked, I saw nothing, nothing at all.

BLUE EYE CREEK

Sometimes it was impossible to see the abandoned old house. But it was there. Billy pointed it out. He and Juan had been frequent visitors and trespassers. Set crooked and dilapidated on the little back road that wound along Blue Eye Creek, which twisted like a tree snake through elm and pine and May flowers crushed beneath the hooves of white-tailed deer.

The two elderly sisters who owned the place were dragged off, one after the other in 1957 and 1959 respectively, into an old-age home by an unforgiving relation, but behind them they left their house and everything in the house was left for everybody else to find. Eventually they made it back, but in coffins, buried together beneath one lone marker set crooked on a hill, the stone, covered in yellow moss in winter, green in summer, and fiery scarlet in autumn.

When the house stood empty, different people found different things in there. A high school girl found a silk bonnet and a dress with petticoats. She had it dry-cleaned and wore it to school. Someone else found an old pipe organ. They hauled it away with rope and planks of wood. There were sealed jars filled with plums, pears, and tomato relish. The white labels edged in red bore water marks and the brown, tired stains of age.

The front door of the house fell off its hinges and in the winter, when the deep snows fell silent through the woods, tramps shared the dark wooden interior with various forest fox and raccoon. Inside, it always smelt musty and wet. Yellowed newspapers spread across the rotting wood floorboards like carpet. By spring, when March winds blew the last snow from the sloping roof and the tramps dispersed, the old house had little left to offer. The roof sagged precariously until one early blustery storm tore a hole through it, forcing it to collapse in upon itself, like the sails of a little boat forgotten, drifting along, the hull wrecked onto an anonymous shore.

During the early winter of 1973 Billy and Juan enjoyed spending quality time with the Terry twins when old snow drifts still hugged the roadside melting in the slow strong late spring sunlight. They found the abandoned house near Paxton Creek to experiment. The sisters were as identical and as willing as a two-cent stamp. They wore matching clothes, cotton underwear with tiny purple flowers, and even sounded alike. Billy and Juan argued about this.

'I was with Cindy,' said Juan.

'I thought I was,' said Billy.

'You were with Susie,' said Juan.

'Wasn't that Cindy?' said Billy.

'Who gives a fuck as long as we got fucked?'

Juan will go to Harvard and earn a Bachelor's Degree in Philosophy and I will go for a walk.

I'd forgotten about the old house decaying but I wanted to remember it, so I trudged through the woods following the path of the little creek, encrusted here and there with packed ice and snow but always visible beneath, clear water glittering. The house was gone. The bright patch of hilltop doused in light, shadow, and dark trees was gone. It was a bald piece of earth, flattened by heavy machinery. Nothing ever stays the same. But the house will always stand in my head. Rickety like the two old sisters, one bent over a cane, one watching out the window, blue-white snow quietly blowing between the pines. And him hidden away, silent, fox-like, eating bean soup out of a can, sucking on lemon drops, drinking the creek water. Waiting to return, all those years later, when he thought nobody would remember, when it was all but forgotten.

THE ROAD TO CRAZY

'They are all fire ants. I can wave a blowtorch, set them alight, listen for the crackle of tiny bodies; they ignite into a feathery curl of dark smoke.'

I asked my brother I said, 'Who are all fire ants?'

'You, me, and everyone we know,' he said.

'And who did you see down by the river?'

He said, 'Colonel Sanders.'

I said, 'No!'

He said, 'Yes! I saw Colonel Sanders sitting in an old Buick by the river, carrying a blowtorch.'

By early 1974 Billy saw all the planets and stars come crashing down on the sidewalk. He could walk on the moon. He said he heard God whisper in his ear. He will grow a goatee. He will wear a felt hat with a high crown. The hat will crush his long curls down the length of his neck and frame his pale but beautiful face. His voice will deepen and his chest will broaden like the river in places. He will talk to me about the secret habits of fish in the river, the air-breathing one and the one with a flat head that can grow twice the length of a man. He believed in the powers nobody else seemed to believe in anymore. He put things in his mouth I didn't understand. Pieces of bark from a wild cherry or the acorns from a chestnut tree he'd crush and toss in a stream, he said, 'this makes the fish dizzy, makes them easier to catch.' Yet he always threw the fish back. Billy said Rattle Box purified blood and Jimson Weed would cure a headache. He knew about Wild Carrot, Toothwart, and Pearly Everlasting. He said if a bird wound a human hair through its nest, the person would lose their mind. I'd say, 'where do you hear all this?' and Billy said, 'From an Indian.'

'No,' I said.

'Yes.'

'What's he look like?'

'Like an Indian,' he said.

I can't say I understood every little thing that made Billy Sycamore tick. I can hardly figure out a trout's motivation let alone half the people I know.

He told me he met a man from the Six Nations with a boiled wool jacket. The man, a full-blooded Indian, said, 'You can journey with the dead only so far then you must turn back. Do you understand?'

'No,' said Billy, 'I don't.'

Then we would go fishing. Along that part of the river that flowed nearest to our house.

THE BIG LEAP

By late summer 1974 I finally found out what Billy had done. Around the time of the Big Leap across the Snake River Canyon when America was crazy about a man who had the most bones broken of any single person in a lifetime. He had already hurtled on a motorcycle over two mountain lions and twenty-feet of rattlesnakes. He jumped the water fountains in Las Vegas and a tankful of lemon sharks in Chicago. He didn't die going over the Grand Canyon. Yet the whole notion of the impending stunt made my mood darken, made my heart clutch. I'd wake up in the middle of the night thinking about wind speeds and trajectory. I'd think about the edge.

Towering sunflowers growing beneath a tall drift of blue pine trees couldn't keep my attention. Billy nailing a four by four piece of plywood over his bedroom window could not hold my attention.

'You expecting someone?'

Yes he said, he was.

But all this changed comet-like. Bang in the centre of our world it blew a hole right threw the roof of our minds when we found out about Billy. I listened to the fall-out: smashing stars, clouds and carbon gases.

When I left Billy's room I had walked past our parents' bedroom. I stood in their doorway long enough to change my life. I had not intended to have a perception shift; originally I was just asking for ten dollars to go to the mall with my best bad friend Tawny Milford, who didn't need money because she stole everything. But sometimes conversations can do that, even one as small as a dime.

I was as visible as daylight but they couldn't see me. And

while listening to them I didn't once think about the Snake River Canyon.

'Did he steal something?' asked our mother.

'No,' said our dad.

'Is he on heroin? He did something to the Stanleys!' It was like watching a television game show from hell. Her hands flew to her mouth. 'He's joined the Moonies!'

He shook his head, our dad.

And then: 'He isn't gay – is he?'

When our father finally told her that Billy shot and killed somebody by the river she said, 'Well don't tell anybody,' followed by, 'I have to play tennis now.'

I carried this knowledge around with me from that moment on like a dark stream in my pocketbook. Sometimes it sprang a leak like fluid panic. I imagined people looking at me. They'd say, 'You've got a hole in your bag. It's leaking river water.'

'I know,' I said.

'Don't you want to get it fixed?'

And I'd think about that question, because it was a good and fair one.

'Yes,' I'd tell them. 'It's just not my river to repair.'

PROLOGUE TO SALT LICK CREEK

It's late October 1975 and the dark has come early. Billy is in his last year of high school while I'm a sophomore who still can't legally drive so he's picking me up from Tawny Milford's house – a two-bedroom stone-rendered house she shares with her ageing parents. Because her parents felt guilty about having her when they were old they gave her everything they couldn't afford – which was a sacrifice for them because they both earned minimum wage working in a dog food factory.

Billy drove our dad's Buick Riviera. The car had a pointy hood and sunroof. Deep maroon with red velvet interior. It looked like the Devil's waiting room. Billy leans on the horn to signal for me to hurry the hell up out of Tawny's house, while she follows behind me into the chilly October night wearing nothing but a bright pink bikini. She wanted to say hi to Billy. She had a big crush on him. She'd quiz me on his likes and dislikes: 'Football?'

'Yes.'

'Beer?'

'Pot.'

'Grateful Dead?'

'Little Feat.'

'Sex?'

'I wouldn't know.'

Tawny's leaning into the driver's side window; she's shaking her double D boobs all over the steering wheel. 'How's it going, Billy?' she askes him.

'Yeah, great,' he said while putting the car in reverse. He cut a sharp right at Montfort Street, obviously unimpressed. She could have done a headstand naked with one hand while playing the kazoo with the other and Billy would be indifferent. It's just how he was these days: depressed, moody, *indifferent.* On the other hand he liked to drive fast.

When we were on the road I said to my brother as my heart rode shotgun: 'It's 35 miles here. Why are you doing 90?'

Billy flew the car like a madman on a Persian carpet winging through the darkness. We were on Old Hickory Lane, forested and twisted, with its flowing dips and uncanny curves cut in the Pleistocene Age by glacial ice inching between the Blue Ridge Mountains, where nice teenagers like us die all the time when they make sharp and reckless turns and hit a tree or a telephone pole.

'You notice?' I said.

'Notice what?' said Billy.

'Now the police are after us,' I said. The black and white patrol car had put on its siren and flashing lights. I could see them speeding up in the side mirror.

'Yes, but I can outrun them,' said Billy.

'Oh Billy – no,' I said.

He floored the car. The police did the same.

I did a quick assessment of the situation and decided if we didn't crash and die I had less to worry about as Billy was driving and would have to take the blame for this one. Therefore I could just sit back in fear and hope for the best.

'Hold on,' he said, as we raced up the hill close to our house with the police not far behind.

Billy swung right and drove straight by our house. Then he pulled into a neighbour's driveway, cutting the car lights and the engine and telling me to, 'Get down' while smashing my face into the velvet seat.

Seconds later the officer of the law went zooming past. Billy backed out of the neighbour's driveway and, with no headlinghts, drove calmly along our street, pulling into our driveway and into our garage, calmly pressing the electric button to close the garage door, as if we'd just driven thoughtfully home from church.

SALT LICK CREEK

Whenever my brother could, he would give away his car. On these occasions he'd either a. stopped taking his medication or b. the medication needed adjustment or c. he would mix the medication with large quantities of beer and reefer which set the very precise nature of the medication askew, and he would give away his car. Like the women in the imagination of a bored middle-aged husband, the prostitutes by the Susquehanna River were actually friends of my brother. He knew girls who worked off Route 17, the road lined with cheap motels, at least two Dunkin Donuts, a Dairy Queen and a Knife World. If you continue north on Route 17, eventually you would get to the source of the Susquehanna River, all the way to Cooperstown, New York, past Salt Lick Creek. However, it would be in Adults Triple X, where my brother would meet the lucky beneficiaries of several of his cars. One stripper got a Dodge Omni, another, the Buick Skylark, and a girl who did odd things with a ballpoint pen; she got the Pontiac Grand Am. This did not please our father, of course, who was the one buying the cars. But the consolation was that our father liked shopping for cars. Our dad would visit ten different Dodge dealers or eight different Chevy dealers, or twelve importers of Nissan cars. He read up on all the latest statistics concerning fan belts, radiators, and transmission. One fine autumn day, my brother and his medication were both adjusted and he was driving along the Susquehanna River going south, and his old Buick Skylark was going north and they crossed paths like two river barges, when Billy recognised his car. Not as in a 'hey that's the goddamned car I gave away when I was out of my head,' but in a, 'I used to have a car like that… yeah, I did…' and then, 'I wonder what ever happened to it?'

MALL OF AMERICA

By December I didn't have to potentially die in my brother's car anymore. I had passed my driver's test and the first thing Opal Pike asked me for was a favour. The favour was Glonell: '*Take* her to the mall which you – she is gettin' on my *last* nerve.'

Teenagers in America liked to hang around the mall to see who else was hanging around the mall. One million square foot of wide-open space on two levels – marble-floored, glass-vaulted and steel-beamed – our mall was the biggest and most exciting thing to happen to Caulderton since the Great Flood.

However I would have rather drunk all the water out of Billy's aquarium than take Glonell to the mall. But before I could protest she'd already jumped into the front seat of the Cadillac, buckled herself in, and then pressed her face against the window like Marvin the dog.

'She do love the mall,' Opal said leaning halfway out the door that led into the garage.

'Whatchu gonna buy me?' Glonell asked, playing with the electric windows as I pulled out.

'Nothing,' I said.

We flew past verdant farmland and the Dairy Queen. We barrelled by the 7-11 and the High School, past Delman's Creek flowing underneath a little bridge where soft, spongy, earth surrounded by wild violets cushioned the noise of the stream of traffic overhead.

'You gotta buy me somethin',' she said.

'I'll think about it,' I told her.

Twenty minutes later I parked the car in front of J.C. Penny's and had it all figured out.

'I'll buy you a pack of Sugar Babies if you always stay at

least three feet in front of me.' As soon as the words had fallen from my mouth she grabbed onto my hand like a bear trap.

Therefore to avoid bumping into anybody I knew, I made sure to bypass the main hub filled with pinball machines and my high school associates such as the effervescent Todd Wertz – who was so good-looking it was hard to look at him. I figured it would be best to take the elusive, more circuitous route, through one of the large department store's normally empty furniture departments which led out to the sunlit second floor and Woolworths. Tawny Milford worked at the Piercing Pagoda. I slunk by as it was opposite the entryway to Woolworths. If she saw me hanging around the mall with Glonell she'd never let me live it down.

There was a pre-Christmas sale going on at Woolworths and Glonell had to touch *everything*: the switches on a blender; she tried to cut off two of her fingers with an electric knife. In another aisle she found a can of instant spray snow for Christmas trees which I managed to wrestle away from her just as she popped the lid. She pried the blinking lights off a reindeer display and I just about had a heart attack when the whole thing toppled over and dropped on her head. A few shoppers looked at us appalled.

Glonell freed herself from the tangle and ran down the bag and suitcase aisle pressing the flip-locks on every piece of luggage.

'You're gonna get us thrown out of here,' I said.

She stuck her tongue out at me.

She tried on diamond rings for $19.97. She set all the clocks in the electronics department to midnight. She went like a demon through neatly folded rows of women's underwear. She put a big pink bra on her head and made me laugh. In the toy department I had to plead with her to get out of a two-man canoe.

After make-up, shampoo, and sanitary napkins, we turned down the candy aisle.

'You gotta buy me them Sugar Babies.'

'Alright,' I said as a hand gripped my shoulder. I whipped around hoping it wouldn't be anybody I knew, and discovered the hand belonged to the Woolworths' security guy. He had on highly polished black shoes. His powder-blue, short-sleeved shirt had armpit stains. He had a walkie-talkie strapped to his belt.

'I'll have to inspect your bag, miss,' he said.

It was a dark brown suede shoulder bag with long fringe. He tried to take it from me. I wouldn't let him. 'Why? What have I done?'

He didn't reply. Instead he got on his walkie-talkie to request assistance, he said, for a 'shoplifter'.

'Just let me check your bag,' said the security guard. 'If there's no contraband you are free to go.'

By this time a small crowd of the curious and nosey gathered to stare. I noticed Glonell had joined them.

I flung the bag towards him. 'You won't find anything,' I said. I had never stolen from a shop. Not even a gum drop. On the other hand Tawny Milford went to New York City on a tenth-grade art trip and returned with a hand-embroidered halter top from Bergdorf's.

'You bought this?' I asked.

'Stole it,' she said. 'I wish I could wear it but my boobs are too big.'

Last Easter Tawny's parents sent her to Europe. They had to work double shifts at the dog food factory – overtime, nights and weekends – just to pay for the trip. Mae Lacey and I went too; an organised eleventh grade class journey but I shared a room with Tawny. We had a lot of laughs except for the very last night, before we were due to fly back to America when she had a realisation.

'Oh, my God,' she said.

'What?' I asked. We were lying on twin beds blowing smoke rings at the ceiling.

'I don't have a present for my parents.'

'Buy them chocolates.'

'Not good enough,' she said. 'They worked *so* hard to send me on this trip I need to have something good to give back.'

Of course Tawny had used all of her spending money to buy clothes and gifts for herself as well as an ashtray with a repeating image of the Eiffel Tower.

'So give them an ashtray.'

'They don't smoke.' During the conversation Tawny was staring at a sweet little painting hanging over her side of the bed. It was a French pastoral scene in watercolours with peasants and cows.

'I should get them a painting,' she said.

'A painting would be nice,' I said. 'But if you don't have any more money then I'd stick with the candy.'

This is when Tawny sat up, removed the painting off the wall, pried off the back, rolled it up and put it in her suitcase. Then she put the empty frame back on the wall.

'I feel much better now,' she said.

I noticed the Woolworths' security guard derisively snorted at every item in my bag when he held it aloft: A pack of silver Christmas tinsel; a miniature sled with a plastic Santa and all his reindeer; a pair of size 18 ladies rayon peach-coloured underpants and a diamond ring for $19.97.

More onlookers had gathered, like I was an accident on the interstate. 'This is a mistake,' I exclaimed pointing to Glonell.

'She stole everything but she was born like this so it's not exactly her fault, I mean – she can't help it.'

A collective gasp of judgemental disgust rose from the crowd; the security guard shook his head like he had caught me eating Marvin's dog food while I looked to Glonell for support but she was clicking her tongue in shame, shaking her head from side to side with the others. 'Oh, my God, she's lying! Can't you see? Just look at her.' I must have sounded pretty crazy because a woman standing just behind Glonell laid a protective arm across her; all they could see was a broken down little child with an uneven jaw and thick eyeglasses. The guard had pinned my arms behind my back.

I noticed Tawny's parents had hung the painting in their kitchen so at every meal they could enjoy the French peasants and cows. In early June Tawny's parents got a call from the school. The hotel had traced our high school group – specifically Tawny and I to the room with the empty picture frame – and Tawny and her parents had to bring the painting into the principal's office. The next time I went to Tawny's house, in place of the French rural scene, hung an oversized calendar from Schlenk Auto.

The Woolworths' security guy marched me towards the back of the store, to a door marked 'Security' while I said: 'She has problems.' I sounded like my parents trying to explain Billy to the Stanleys and why he stood outside that time, in the middle of a snowstorm, watering their front flower bed wearing nothing but a ski hat.

WHEN THE INDIANS OWNED
THE BINGO HALL

By September 1975 Billy had left for college. He was going to the University of Michigan to study Liberal Arts because he didn't know what else to study. He said he'd miss seeing Joseph Lightfoot who saw his Indian ancestors all the time. He told Billy he could see them just before a storm broke free like a wild horse, when the whole sky was charged up like one enormous vibrating arrow.

'You believe that?' I asked Billy.

'I believe it,' said Billy, 'We don't know the half of it.'

Joseph Lightfoot told Billy Sycamore all about Indian rights and wrongdoings. He told Billy his forefathers owned the Bingo Hall, Food Land, and Wexler's Auto Supply. All of downtown and the West Bridge Mall.

'If you think about it objectively,' said Joseph Lightfoot, 'Of course I own all that real estate.'

Now not too far from the Susquehanna River and about two hundred years earlier a meeting took place between the Indians of the Six Nations and the Commissioners from Maryland and Virginia. The Commissioners wanted to send some Indian braves to college. The Indian chiefs said the last time they participated in a cultural exchange their team returned ineffectual. They came back with their hair cut poorly and dressed in a cheap suit and tie. They became lousy runners, fisherman, hunters and counsellors. The chiefs said: 'Basically they are totally good for nothing.'

By late November Billy came back from college ineffectual. I don't know how long it took for the Indian braves to have their equilibrium eradicated but it took my brother about three months, or by the middle of the first semester we found him – well, actually Marvin the dog found him – under the kitchen table. He wasn't doing much there.

'Hey, Billy,' I said. I bent down to see he wasn't wearing any clothes. I decided to talk to him from the chair at the other end.

'What's new?'

'Nothing,' he said.

Lying beside Billy, like a pet snake, was a 12-gauge shotgun and a canvas duffle bag. I wondered what was in the bag.

Billy looked both outraged yet unexcitable all at once. I wasn't sure which road in this odd-forked moment he was going to choose, and if it was the former I didn't want to be in line of sight of the gun.

When Billy went to college three months ago it was a sign he was normal – or at least okay; and all of this mental mania a kink or phase. Besides, I had on my cheerleading uniform; I didn't want to have to go to a football game now and jump around with pom poms, pretending all is vacuous and wonderful with the world when my brother is sitting at home naked under the kitchen table with a shotgun.

'Did something happen at college?'

'No,' he said. 'Why do you ask?'

My uniform had a giant red Indian head on the chest. Our high school colours were red and black. Joseph Lightfoot told Billy our high school was a bunch of unenlightened racial motherfuckers. 'Does my skin look red?' he'd ask.

'Only when you're drinking,' said Billy.

The grandfather clock chimed half past four.

'Are you going to be ok?' I ask him.

'Why?'

'I don't know – you might want some clothes.' He placed his hand on the duffle bag.

'What's in the bag?' I asked.

'The chicken guy.'

I knew who Billy meant. This was not good.

Not good at all.

HEY, BROTHER

When our ancestors still lived along the River Taff, or in some dark Welsh village by the sea, people were running away by the Susquehanna River. They bundled up their heartbeats and dreams and fled into the rapids and torrents of life. Sometimes the wind blew their heads adrift, thoughts and prayers floating above violet hills and lemon-coloured fields. Then they would sit down on a strange rock.

Sometimes they would catch the same fish twice, its lip hanging off, a little to the right, or to the left, like a poorly hung painting, and they'd say, 'Hey, brother, I know you…'

Along the Susquehanna River, which means 'Muddy River,' in a deviated Indian language, a merger of Iroquoi and Susquehannock, there is a hospital with a bright psychiatric ward. In the psychiatric ward there are nurses and doctors and patients, all interchangeable. Like pieces in a strange puzzle a child could arrange, the nurses placate the patients, the doctors placate the nurses, the patients are out of their heads on all sorts of medication or else supine, fish on a slab, restrained by leather straps. It is that kind of super efficiency and one out-of-tune piano, a community room with a television, a candy and soda machine, and books like: *How German Is It?* And *Black Pow Wow* that define this particular psychiatric ward. And when things stop working in Billy's head, like an alarm clock somebody forgot to rewind, he will hear disembodied voices. He will drool in his sleep. He will start to wear thick eyeglasses. He will run away from the Susquehanna River. 'I must have a brain tumour,' he said.

One doctor, wearing a Harvard School tie, asked Billy if he thought the President of Mexico was trying to contact him through his dental work. Billy thought this pretty unlikely, and the question itself deserved a huge round of applause so he said the President of Mexico does try to contact him then proceeded to tune a radio dial in his ear.

The psychiatrist wrote something down on a yellow legal pad. 'And what does the President of Mexico tell you?' he asked.

Nuestras vidas son los rios
que van a dar en el mar, (he said).

The psychiatrist did not find this amusing at all and he told Billy he was a busy man and he should take clinical depression (that's what they said he had) more seriously. But it seemed more urgent than that, less flowery, particularly as he started to carry a huge Christian cross around in the back pocket of his blue jeans, and that's pretty psychiatric for a Jew.

Our lives are the rivers
that run into the sea

He told the psychiatrist, he said: 'I killed a Civil War General by the river. Now, you want to talk about crazy?'

which is death…

All this coming and going and sinking away, into the gently flowing waters, out to sea.

A BEWILDERING NET

It is a late Friday afternoon in February 1976 and we are sitting in the common room on the tenth floor of the psychiatric ward visiting Billy.

The Susquehanna River is still frozen in places. When the warmer winds blow and the sun grows stronger the water level will rise. People who live along the river get river-worry, they wonder if it will flood this year and the waters carry off their furniture. About two per cent of the three and a half million miles of rivers in America are free-flowing. The rest are damned or short-circuited, much like Billy.

'Did you know fish can drown?' Billy asks me. He had a nervous breakdown last autumn. Too much acid dropped at college; too much bad brain chemistry made for this moment now.

He exists in a hazy kind of reality, bloated and sad-faced. A beautiful fish caught in a bewildering net.

In all of his psychotic glory, like a stained-glass window shattered and glued back together more than once, I love my brother Billy.

'They can you know... drown. In the nets, they get caught. Listen to me, Alice,' he whispers: '*I'm drowning.*'

Billy's been here since Christmas when he finally got out from under the kitchen table and started to copy *Roget's Thesaurus* all over his bedroom walls in dark purple crayon.

He began with *Abstract Relations* until he reached *Unrelatedness* – all wildly written: row upon jagged row of relative and opposite words before he was caught by Opal who had come into his room one afternoon to run the sweeper, looked around and said, 'If you think I'm gonna clean all this off, then you really *is* crazy.'

Our mother is here too, looking pensive in a dark mink coat. Her brunette hair matched the coat. She wears lavender eye shadow and her shoes have an insane buckle of an American eagle. I am in my cheerleading uniform. I've been a cheerleader since September. If it was a regular job I would have already been fired. I forget the cheers. I forget the pom poms. The biggest, meanest cheerleader on the squad threatened to "kick my butt" if I didn't start cheering right.

That's what she said, 'You better start cheering right or I'm gonna kick your butt.'

I thought cheerleading was supposed to be a friendly pastime. I had no idea it could be so violent and oppressive.

We are only allowed into the community room of the psychiatric ward, and we have to stand here smiling at all the psychotics, who are seated around several low white tables, the kind used by small schoolchildren.

Billy is dressed in faded jeans and a blue and green flannel shirt. His hands are trembling. He's sitting next to a young girl with a long, dreary face who looks like a dead woman eating a candy bar. She seems to me a whole mystery entombed in a dainty kind of violence. Of course my brother likes her. I can tell. Sisters can tell those sorts of things about their brothers. She has beautiful shining black hair sweeping all the way down to her waist. I stand there admiring her hair. I know she is crazy and I only want her hair. She sits to the left of my brother who says, 'This is Angel.' She says nothing.

My brother starts around the table introducing each and every person like the ambassador of some obscure and odd island home, and these people worked for the State Department there.

A black girl was studying a fly on the ceiling. There was a man with a buzz-saw haircut and eyebrows like two gazelles leaping. He stared at my cheerleading outfit. He scrutinised the gigantic Indian head sewn onto the black jumper; the short red skirt; the red and black striped knee socks, the black and white saddle shoes then he said to me: *What are you in for?* Still I couldn't admit to myself my brother belonged here anymore than I belonged on a cheerleading squad – Tawny Milford had put me up to it, talked me into trying out: 'C'mon,' she said, 'let's do it for a laugh.' I got picked, she didn't.

Our mother tried to make small talk with Angel. Maybe she thought this could be her future-daughter-in-law. 'What do you like to do, Angel?' Our mother smiled brightly.

'Pull the wings off flies then watch them turn in circles.'

I hoped she couldn't see the one on the ceiling.

In Africa, there is a giant flying termite. A red ant-type caterpillar with wings that are clear. One day I will see their wings. Hundreds of thousands of them, littering the earth, and the inside of a house, like a transparent fairy carpet. When the rains come, the Africans stand under street lights pulling off the wings and eating the ants. But they are still a termite underneath.

I just wasn't sure if my brother was the same underneath.

When there was nothing else possible on earth to say, my mother said: 'It was just so nice to meet you all,' like she's been at a bridge luncheon and not the mental ward. Yet there seemed no rightness, no wrongness, and no absolutes here; just sadness, just my brother, and all the mental and emotional problems he's starting to conjure up in every conceivable angle, size, and contortion.

BILLY'S GIRLFRIEND

It's early May and Billy's got a girlfriend. He met her through the mental health system out-patient clinic when he got released last month and she has five brothers. They range in size, age, emotional problems and varying pending legal wrangles. They are the Jesse James of brothers. They all have long, dry beards, ride motorcycles and eat at the Parkside Diner.

Billy's already endured a couple of electroshock therapy treatments during his incarceration; and afterwards, he couldn't remember his name or if he had any long-range goals. 'It's not quite the electric chair,' he said, 'but I seem to be moving in that direction.'

The river is here but nobody can see it. The view is blocked by parked cars and two policewomen pounding at the girlfriend's door.

'Aren't you going to get the door?' Billy asks.

'I am not,' she says.

The police are threatening to return with a crowbar. She taunts them: 'You just try,' she yells. 'They're all bastards,' she says.

This Jesse James of a girlfriend is not physically handicapped yet parks her ten-year-old Toyota in the spaces reserved for the handicapped and refuses to pay the fines when she's caught. She owes this little town, between river and mountaintop, a hell of a lot of money.

'My car don't always work right,' she says drinking a can of beer before 11am, 'it's handicapped.'

I met her on a beautiful afternoon, and the first thing she said was, 'You look skinnier than I thought you'd look. You wanna root beer?'

The second thing she said was: 'D'ya fish?'

I am about to answer when Billy comes inside. He's found a frog in an outdoor toilet. He shows the girlfriend who gets very excited. She rubs the top of the terrified frog's noggin and says, 'Let's keep it!'

I think she can't be all bad then in the next breath she says: 'I know somebody in prison. You know anybody in jail?'

Billy's girlfriend lives in a little farmhouse with a sagging roof and sinking foundations. She sits on the edge of the world and says, 'a glass on the kitchen table is starting to slide southward.'

She sips root beer mixed with bourbon out of an old grape jelly jar. She grins at Billy. Her teeth flying all over her mouth; a kite in the wind. She has a thick body, short arms and man-sized feet. I couldn't figure out what my brother is doing with her. I tell myself Billy is on so many meds he probably thinks she's Miss America.

'We got a lot in common,' she says, reading my mind. I look over at my brother sitting in a haze. She had a child by one of her five brothers, when she was fourteen.

We knew all about incest from Bonnie Noland, a girl whose father used to creep into her bedroom at night and do terrible things. In the ninth grade, when she couldn't hide her six-month pregnancy any longer, the school nurse asked who was responsible and she said, 'Chad Everett.'

That Chad Everett came into her room every night. And the nurse, who wasn't born yesterday, called social services and the Nolands moved to Colorado the following month, without Mr Noland, who got ten years without parole.

'You'd get along real good with my brother, Chet,' she tells me pulling out a photo. There are five bull-necked men, all with the same long reddish beards and matching bowl haircuts. She tapped the one on the far right. The one holding the bloodied deer head by its antlers. The rest of the deer's body was straddled by a barefoot Chet in farmer jeans.

'He likes 'em skinny,' she said then added, 'I used to be skinny 'fore the baby.'

I wanted to kill my brother, right then and there.

THE FISH IN THE WOODS THAT WALKED TO THE RIVER

We drove past Bill's Bait & Tackle and the strange old man with the great flowing beard who sits beneath the Lincoln Avenue bridge and picks invisible things out of his teeth. We flew past people waiting at the Thurmont ferry that cuts through long, dreamy streams of river grass, growing so shallow you can jump off the boat in the middle of the river and walk the rest of the way to shore, to go fishing. He has a sweatband on his wrist and a regulation US Army canvas bag slung across the vest he wears with twenty-seven pockets. Billy's in a good mood; having just visted his petulant girlfriend who is crazier than he is.

'What have you got in your pockets?' I ask him.

'Lunch,' he says, 'and a fantastic calm.'

He's had several shock therapy treatments in the last several months and part of his brain seems to be functioning at a peculiar angle.

'What are we walking around in here for?' I ask. 'The river is behind us.'

The American Sycamore is the same tree whether referred to by its scientific name, *Platanus Occidentalis*, or you call it a Sycamore. It has the same ovate-shaped leaf with tooth-edged margins, and the bark, a mottled brown and white will turn grey and scaly like a fish when it becomes old.

In the woods there is a creek. In winter it will become the snow on the mountain. In spring it will become the melt water that fills the river.

Behind the river is something else. In the woods there is a path full of shadow and leaf where the mayflower blooms for a short time each spring. The air smells full of decay, damp leaves, and dark soil. There is suspended here an eternity creeping along the forest floor. It is the same as the current that pushes the river forward and the root system growing downward and the limbs of everything moving upwards, and the energy held within every single star, within every exhale.

I see a switchblade in my brother's back pocket. Billy is not to have the switchblade in his pocket. In fact, Billy is not to have knives or guns or lighter fluid anymore. The following had to be confiscated:

A Thompson submachine gun
A Magnum .357 (with a silencer)
A Colt .45 (the commemorative edition which was sold to a crazy radiologist, who moved to Florida)
A military pistol in a velvet case (worth a small fortune and re-sold to Bullet Barn.)
2 BB guns.

There are great vines growing all around in a tangle, and trumpet flowers now closed until tomorrow. The river is behind us and it is getting darker and cooler and the sky has disappeared. The molecules are bursting with invisible waterfalls and the river is full of fish and dark water. The deeper you go, the darker the water.

My brother stops. I stop. He's just standing still. Everything is silent. I don't hear any leaves stir or animals move in the underbrush. The birds have flown off.

'Did you hear that?' Billy asks.

'Hear what?'

He holds an index finger to his lips. I can just about catch the inner workings of Billy's mind striking, the heart of an old grandfather's clock inside his chest on the second-storey landing. Sheer black curtains hang in a great curved-arch window.

Everything in here feels ionised. It smells electric.

'This is crazy,' I say.

'I am crazy,' he says.

Everything feels slow motion and worrisome, stuck in the woods with my brother and his brain chemistry.

It might be okay. The day might be okay. But I don't think so, on the path where everything smells dry but damp inside. There are molecules all over us bursting with invisible waterfalls. Towering above, white oak, maple, sycamore, and pitch pine bring the sky down.

'You aren't going to do anything regrettable?' I ask.

'Shut up,' he says.

'You shut up,' I say.

Billy's looking at something.

'What is it?'

But Billy is silent.

I push him aside to see what he sees. Our brains could not make sense of it. We shook our heads.

Later I said: 'What did your girlfriend put in the root beer?'

We ran until all sound returned: the wind, the birds, and the whistle of a train running along the edge of the mountain, its cars filled with refrigerators, easy chairs, and cocoa beans.

Nobody in their right mind sees a fish walk down to the river.

'You saw it – and don't lie,' he says.

'What? – A man in waders and a wetsuit?' I said, just to be the sane one.

'No, Alice,' said Billy with the conviction of a television evangelist – 'it's evolution gone loco.'

111

And I often wondered if the strange lights people keep seeing near the river aren't space-fish dropped off by UFOs.

And I often wondered if mental illness was as contagious as a summer cold.

DELMAN'S CREEK

In the old people's home near Delman's Creek is a ninety-nine-year-old woman lying in a small iron bed. She has watery green eyes and white hair. She's watching *The Gong Show*.

Our high school volunteers at the old people's home to get extra credit for Civics class and I'm one of the volunteers.

'You're not watching the *Praise the Lord Club*?' asked a care home worker.

'That crap? It's for the birds,' she said.

The ninety-nine-year-old woman would like to die. Whenever I see her, I say: 'How are you?' And she always says the same thing: 'Not so good. I'd like to die already.'

There is a photo album that is never very far from her.

'Give me that,' she points with a gnarled old hand. Her fingers are knotted tree roots. She yanks open the photo album and points to people who are strangers to me but familiar to her.

'See that one?' she says.

'I do,' I say.

'A bitch,' she says.

'Really?' I say.

'A bitch from hell,' she says.

The woman to whom she is referring is looking sideways at the camera. She is seated at a long table with flowers arranged in the centre.

'Is she still alive?' I ask knowing full-well she is dead, because the last time I was here, I saw the same photo and got the same speech.

'Dead,' says the ninety-nine-year-old woman with white hair, 'dead and buried, since 1971.'

'That's sad,' I say.

'Sad it is not! She made up lies about me, jealous lies.'

Then the old woman spat into an aquamarine plastic tub.

'Let me show you something else,' she said.

'Okay,' I said, but I know what she is going to show me. We go through this routine every time I come here.

She pulls back a light blue sheet and yellow cotton blanket. I see the white nylon underwear of a ninety-nine-year-old woman who wants to die. But her legs are the legs of a much younger woman.

'You have beautiful legs.'

'You're damned right I do,' she says and, 'Now you tell me something.'

I told the old woman I could hear voices singing through the trees, that the fish are my friends, I ask them for things. One time I asked a fish for a boyfriend, another time, a pocketbook. I told her my brother and I saw a fish walk down to the river.

At this the old woman began to laugh. She grabbed a fistful of her nightgown with her tree root fingers

She laughed so hard her beautiful old legs began to tremble, and her face grew dark and veined, like mist, hard shale and stone, spattered by raindrops.

EARTH BATTERIES

The economic structure of our town is straightforward. You've either got old money, new money, or no money. To keep from having no money when he was released from the psychiatric unit Billy was going to sell Holy Water by mail order. He wanted to put the Susquehanna River in clear plastic bottles shaped like the Virgin Mary. Juan Goldstein, who was home from Harvard for the summer said they'd do better selling lightning rods. Juan wanted to market 'Earth Batteries' – buried galvanized plates. This, he said, would dispel a lightning bolt into the air.

'How do you know all this?' Billy asked.

'I've been talking to some people,' Juan said, 'mostly at Radio Shack.'

'Okay,' said Billy, 'let's go.'

On an overcast afternoon threatening rain they followed the line of the train tracks in an old pick-up truck all the way to the steelworks. The steelworks had been shut down. It was opened in 1866 and it worked a long hard time. It made pig iron and the pig iron made rich people richer and working-class people work harder. Then the steelworks shut down. There wasn't enough money to run things anymore. It's a big fossil now, sitting next to the river and the train tracks.

They parked the truck by a row of two-storey houses with fake brick fronts and little pinwheels stuck in the earth turning. To the average person, the slow-talking one with long hair tied back in a lady's hair clip, and the pale-faced and funny-talking Billy, with a goatee and blond afro going door to door selling lightning rods, looked a little odd. But this was in Milroy, in August 1976, and near the old steelworks.

Billy and Juan figured lightning must strike there more than anywhere else in town, on account of all that metal.

Their first job was for a man from the Caribbean in his mid-thirties. He wore a T-shirt that said: I LOVE ST KITTS. 'How much for di whole blam-blam?' he asked.

'Thirty-five dollars,' said Juan.

'Which includes installation,' said Billy.

'Uh-huh. Wen mi come to a decishan,' said the man. He thought about the lightning rod for a whole minute. He was pretty stoned.

'Soh how big is di lightning?' he asked.

'The rod is thirty-foot tall,' said Billy.

He whistled, the man.

The wind was blowing hard. It blew the leaves silver on the row of elm and sugar maple trees lining the sidewalk. Thunder echoed from the direction of Cleota, where only last week a fourteen-year-old boy shot his whole family during dinner. When the police had asked him why he'd done such a fucked-up, psychopathic thing he said, 'I hate meatloaf.'

'We'll run a grounding wire inside the house and connect it to the cold water pipes. This way you won't have wires running up and down the exterior of your house,' said Juan.

The man listened with his head down. He was one of those people who could do that, listen to one person but do something else. He was reading a copy of *TV Guide*. 'An yu sure I can watch mi TV?'

'Sure,' said Juan.

'Sure,' said Billy.

'An yu bonifide?' he asked.

'I've had a short writing stint at WKRON,' said Juan, 'and I can catch arrows with my bare hands.'

'I do a lot of fly fishing,' said Billy, 'and I'm thinking of branching out into antiques.'

'OK,' said the man. 'I'll take mi rod.'

The first thing Billy did when they got onto the roof was stick his foot through the shingles where it made a hole. The second thing Billy did was lean the lightning rod against the TV mast. This would have been alright except for the incoming storm and the lightning bolt, like the finger of God pointing, that struck the ungrounded copper rod and the current travelled, about 10,000 volts, straight down the mast and into the man's living room blowing up his TV. He had been watching a re-run of *McMillan and Wife*. The force blew him out of his chair and across the room where he landed just under the hole in the roof, his hat, striped like an African flag, and his coconut-oiled hair, had combusted from a flying spark. The rain came through the hole and put out the flames before they ignited his eyebrows and beard.

Billy didn't feel the strike. He had jumped off the roof in time because he'd left some bolts in the truck. Juan heard the TV explode, and because he was the Ludwig Wittgenstein of our little town, he deduced within a micro-second he and Billy were responsible.

'I think we've killed our first customer,' he said. They both looked through the picture window to see the man lying on a green shagpile carpet, his scalp steaming.

The boys let themselves in through the front door. Juan felt the man's pulse. Billy listened to his heart. 'He's still ticking,' said Billy. They dragged the man back to his recliner, and arranged him in a position where he was sitting about as upright as anybody unconscious could be, and they stuck the TV remote back in his hand. When the man came to, he couldn't remember his name, his telephone number, or what his long-range goals in life were.

SCHLENK AUTO

In September 1976, during the autumn of my senior year in high school, when Billy should have been entering his sophomore year in college, yet was still sitting around in his bedroom on Canton Street, he discovered something he was good at besides fishing. Selling cars he managed like the wind rushing beneath the wings of a starling.

Soon he was employee of the month. Soon he was employee of the month for five months in a row. He started to wear a suit. He started to wear a tie. And during a three-week manic depressive episode, Billy managed to sell more cars than any other employee in the history of the dealership. Nobody who worked there suspected Billy of any sort of biochemical jangle, even though he conducted his sales' pitches in peculiar voices ranging from a runaway slave to Geronimo. He broke all sales records and the manager of Schlenk Auto wouldn't have cared if Billy was the Devil Himself as long as he kept selling cars.

Sometimes Billy spoke like a televangelist: 'this here car will deliver you and yours whether to the mall or into a thicket of serpents. Let the Audi 200 Turbo guide you.'

'Where did you get *that*?' our dad asked Billy when he drove a gleaming new Audi into our driveway.

'My boss,' said Billy. The boss let Billy drive the car as a reward for being his prized salesperson.

A month later the car was gone.

'Where's the car?' our dad asked. He loved cars as much as Billy.

'They took it back. I'm going to sleep now.'

Billy had done a test drive in the biggest most expensive and flashiest Audi on the lot.

118

A prospective client wanted to see how the car handled on curves and edges, in traffic and on a deserted back road. Billy was only too happy to fly past the old Indian School doing 110 miles an hour – the school once attended by forty different Native Americans who were told to forget who they were. It takes a whole life's journey just to figure out who you are, and the Indian was told to forget all that. Now you are going to be somebody else.

Unfortunately Billy lost control, hit the median strip, flipped three times and landed upright on the shoulder of the highway the car resembling a crushed can more than a high performance automobile. I imagine the passenger must have never seen life in quite the same way again.

Billy slept through most of the spring that year and finished out the summer back at the psychiatric hospital by the river. But he wasn't psychopathic enough to commit on a permanent, throw-the-key away basis.

When Billy came home in late August the first thing our father did was confiscate Billy's psychotropic drug medication and flush it all down the toilet. He said: 'You don't need these anymore. You're fine now.'

But Billy wasn't fine. 'I'm starting to hear voices,' he said.

'As long as they aren't telling you to kill anybody,' said our dad, 'don't worry about them.'

ROLA COLA

In between escalating nervous breakdowns Billy sat around a lot. The purple irises grew by the white painted front door of our fieldstone ranch house, as familiar to him as the deep green lawn, rich and nourished with grass seed. The dark, sweet earth cradled crab apples that fell off the brown branches before the heavy snows blanketed the ground, from late November sometimes through to early May, but Billy hardly noticed as he was stuck in himself, the hands on a clock that has all the mechanisms in place but can't move forward.

It was hard for him to get up.

Sometimes it got so bad he would lie flat on his back and watch water seeping through plasterboard in the ceiling of his bedroom. 'I think sparrows are nesting in there,' he would say.

'Where?' I asked him.

'Up there,' he'd say. I would look but I couldn't picture the birds.

'I can't get up,' he would say.

'Why not?'

'I don't know. I can't put my finger on it.'

When Billy finally got up he walked to Philadelphia to fish in a spot just behind the Museum of Art. He had visions of things that made all the sense in the world to him. He said he could talk to Betsy Ross, who sewed the first American flag. He said he cracked the Liberty Bell with a crowbar. He could walk on the moon.

Then in the late summer some relations stepped in. When relations step in it can be a good thing, or not, and Billy went to live with Raymond and Raymond's family to find out. In the northwest part of the state around Pitt Hole Creek, a slow-moving and bleary-eyed creek like a hangover, the water cool and dark, and home to plenty of wild brown trout. Billy lives with a great uncle he'd never seen in his life, and works in the uncle's bottling plant. He packs Rola Cola onto trucks and takes of Rola Cola off of trucks. He will work with Raymond and some of Raymond's fishing buddies: people out on parole for armed robbery, rape and assault.

Nobody likes to talk about Raymond, but I will. I could talk about him all day long because nobody else makes me and Billy look as good on the family tree.

Billy did mention that he and Raymond used to go fishing. He said they fished the mouth of Potato Creek on the upper reaches where the stream forks. Or else they drove to Oil City in Venango County in Raymond's pick-up, and over to Porcupine Creek. They'd go fly fishing for Steelhead trout after heavy autumn rains pushed the fish out of the lake and into the feeder streams. At Christmas Raymond gave Billy a copy of *Fly Tying Made Clear and Simple*. Billy gave Raymond a lightning rod.

Raymond spoke fluent Russian. He spoke Ancient Greek. He wore farmer jeans with scraps of paper jammed into every pocket.

Nobody knew how deep and dirty the waters of Cousin Raymond stirred.

Our mother only whispers his name now because Raymond is one of those cousins you never think about until a talk-show host opens up the deep freeze in his garage with a crowbar on national television. Now you think about Cousin Raymond all the time.

The FBI want to know what Raymond was doing moving 1,040 pounds worth of debris from the bottling plant, which had long shut down, and dumping it into nearby Lake Beaver.

It's not easy being a beaver. It must have been a whole lot worse when European trappers wanted to wear the poor beavers as coats and hats. They traded beavers for rum with the local Indian populations. The beaver population went into decline as did the Indians from the rum. Billy went into serious decline the night cousin Raymond and Great Uncle Hank took the family pet German shepherd into the backyard. She was old and sick and tired. When dogs get like that, pet owners, in their right and gentle minds, take their ailing dog to the vet.

Billy stood in the cold and the darkness and watched Uncle Hank tie the dog to a tree stump. He saw the gleam of the .22 rifle in the starlight. Billy said he knew she knew.

'How do you know she knew?' I said.

'How can you not know,' he said.

Billy packed his things. He drove all night without stopping. When the car ran out of gas he left it on the I-80 and he walked, in the bleak February freeze, the rest of the way home. Then he stayed in bed for several months.

He said he felt ineffectual.

'You mean good for nothing?' I said.

'You're not helping,' he said.

ALL IN THE MIND

It is November 1978. I am home from a college and I have a boyfriend. I really like my new boyfriend. He likes that I was once a cheerleader. He made me promise to return to college with the pom poms and the skirt.

It's also Thanksgiving week and Billy talked me into dragging a shovel through the woods. Billy often wanders up and down the banks of the river searching for something he wanted badly to find. He'd scour the woods, he'd dig hole after hole by the water's edge. He'd march forwards and backwards in the same leafy and wooded triangle of space, using a compass or a magnifying glass, measuring with pieces of string.

'Where do you want me to start?' I asked him. Billy liked to dig up dead things to see how long it took their bodies to decay and fall apart. He did this with insects and birds, my pet gerbil. It was cold and overcast yet Billy wore a T-shirt and jeans, like it was still mid-August..

'Here,' he said excitedly. 'Right here.' He was standing over a fallen tree stump with a half-buried car tyre.

'What am I looking for?'

'Don't worry about it.'

'How will I know when I find it?'

'You'll just know.'

'Why can't you just say?'

'Because if I tell you then you'll be an accomplice and we'll both fry.' I knew what he meant.

'Nobody's going to the electric chair.'

'I've seen it,' he shouted. 'I saw myself in flames then ash. My bones crumbled and my guts exploded all over the walls. Don't you fucking tell me what I saw or didn't see – you know what? You just don't know, okay? Admit it, you don't have a freakin' clue.'

The psychiatrist our brother saw, a man who wore black suits and a fantastic long white beard said things like, 'There is only good judgment and bad judgment,' but he never would tell Billy which way to judge although at least he narrowed it down for him to two options. On the other hand, the psychiatrist told our parents Billy suffered from heightened anxiety and delusions because Billy was bipolar and schizophrenic; and he did not shoot a man in a Confederate hat by the river.

'All in the mind,' said the psychiatrist, while tapping the side of his own head.

When Billy wasn't excavating the woods or unable to get out of bed he turned manic and methodical in his search for work. He'd circle with thick red marker any and every job he thought he could handle from circus acrobat to truck driver from associate professor in comparative religion to shoe cleaner for a bowling alley. Then a job opened up at Knife World. He had to say, 'Hello, my name is Billy Sycamore and this, (this is where he would hold up a hatchet), is a sassy knife.' He talked in his bipolar and schizophrenic voices when they were available. He sold more luxury cheese knife sets than any other employee. One day he demonstrated the blade on the neck of a rag doll. The rag doll had a sweet, little face. Billy had put the rag doll on a wooden cutting board and pretended to be the Grand Inquisitor from another era. It might have been funny to the customer if the rag doll wasn't black, or the customer.

Billy could have been a ventriloquist, or worked for the circus. His imagination levitated. He was the magical skin of a fish while his soul, dark and pitiful, was caught in a net. He kept trying to find himself, but he looked in all the wrong places. It is a terrible thing never to find yourself: your heart travels down one river, while your mind goes over the waterfall, drowned in pebbled silence.

THE PSYCHIATRIC WARD

He finally did it. He managed to get locked up in the state hospital on a semi-permanent basis in August.

It is Christmas 1978 now and he is handsome but bewildered. Sometimes he looks hard-faced and bitter. He will eat five small oranges every night. He will drink five cans of Pepsi and rot his beautiful teeth. He will speak English with a funny accent. He listens to the inexplicable howling performed by the state Opera of South Korea, and now and then he accidentally swallows pins.

'I have some pains,' he says.

'From what?' I ask.

'Maybe I swallowed a pin.'

'A pin?'

'Yes.'

'Do you do that a lot?' I ask, alarmed.

'No,' he says, 'not a lot.'

Inside the formidable old building, Billy explained, were visible and invisible things. The invisible were sudden shifts of light and motion, all peripheral, skipping to the extreme left or the extreme right, the kind of invisibility that makes a cat arch its back or a dog howl in a corner. The visible included Billy staring into the cold grey linoleum floor tiles. His room has no walls to speak of and he is always visible. There is a single mattress on the floor with bed sheets covered in smiling zoo animals. They are sheets a child would use.

Above is a window. There is a box outside with a great tangle of red geraniums, all green leaves and thickening stems. He tried to jump last week, fifty feet down from such a cheerful ledge. Then he changed his mind. The window overlooks an interior area full of garbage cans and a central metal drain to catch rainwater.

In the building directly opposite is a Japanese man from Baltimore who puts a carton of milk on his window ledge in the evenings. Sometimes when I visit Billy we watch him. He has shiny black hair and a white T-shirt. I am sure he knows we are sitting there staring, but he never stares back.

One day I will have a boyfriend from Japan; a good-looking Japanese alcoholic who will start drinking cans of Schlitz from 6am. Our father will call me a 'traitor'. He will say, 'How can you forget The Long March?' and I will reply, 'He's a drunk, daddy, believe me, he couldn't march to the corner store and back.' The Japanese boyfriend and I will argue. We will disagree over God knows what as I could speak no Japanese and the only thing he will say in English is: 'You crazy.' He will say this over and over, time and again.

A lady janitor is washing the floors. 'I wash the earth,' she tells Billy.

Billy told her about Joseph Lightfoot; how he helped him water the earth. He told her they moved single ton containers of water on the back of a pick-up truck to building sites around town. How they spilled the water onto the earth, rinsing it clean of sawdust and old plaster, nails and debris.

'I wash the earth too,' he says.

Sometimes a quiet, dark-haired, blue-eyed, twenty-three year old drops by and talks to me because I am Billy's sister. She will sit with us while we watch the guy from Baltimore and his cartons of milk. This reminds her of a story, one of those stories that have to do with a person, a frying pan, and a beautiful girl from Pittsburgh.

'He invited the girl from Pittsburgh up to his apartment,'

127

she says, 'he was going to make dinner for her. He took out a frying pan. The girl probably said something like, 'what's for dinner?' and the boy said 'you are', and that's when he strangled her. So he cut off her breasts and fried them in the pan, with olive oil, peppers, and chopped onion. Then he put them on a plate and ate them.'

'What else did he eat?' I asked.

'Just the breasts,' she said.

'How do you know?' I said.

'I lived in the same apartment building,' she said. 'I saw the whole thing from my bedroom window.'

'Didn't you call the police?' I asked.

'No,' she said, 'Why?'

Billy had no walls. He said sometimes he could see a dwarf jogging in place. He said the dwarf was four foot five and stark naked except for his shoes. I asked Billy why the dwarf was there.

'Indecent exposure,' he said.

'What do you miss most?' I asked him because I couldn't think of anything else to ask.

'Walls,' he said.

Then he paused.

'I've fallen on hard times.'

'I'm sorry,' I said.

'Don't be sorry,' he said.

HISTORICAL BATTLES

We are driving along the river in an old Ford station wagon. It's early January 1979 and not even eight in the morning and his father is already asking what my goals in life are. I guess that's what fathers of nice Jewish boys are supposed to ask the new girlfriend.

'Are you a lawyer, a doctor, or a dentist?' the boyfriend's father asks me with a wink 'or are you just *hoping* to marry a lawyer a doctor or a dentist?' he asks with a larger wink.

'I really don't know,' I say.

'You don't know *what* you are or you don't know *what* you want to do – or *some* of the above or *all* of the above?' he asks me.

I hated this man.

My boyfriend's father wants me to sit next to him on a beige sofa in their modest brick house near Conowego Creek. I do not want to sit next to him. I saw what he did in the bus station's cafeteria. This man makes my brother Billy look like the poster child for restraint and emotional stability.

The father who came rushing at us for a group hug looks like Norman Mailer. A beige raincoat unbelted and flapping wildly around him. Then he made us sit down in the bus station cafeteria while he chose a piece of pie in the cafeteria line. He returned with a slice of custard cream pie and three forks. It was rubbery and dusted with nutmeg. My boyfriend wanted the bite of pie at the beginning, the little pie point. The father wanted that bite too, apparently, because he pinned his kid's hand down to the table with a fork while the boy began to scream.

The carpet beneath our feet is beige. The walls are beige. On the coffee table is a pack of matches from the Geronimo Hotel and next to the matches is a photo album. The father picks up the photo album.

'Let me introduce you to the rest of our family,' he said.

'Okay,' I said.

'Have you got any brothers or sisters?' he asked.

'I have an older brother, Billy Sycamore.'

'And what does Billy Sycamore do?' the father asked me.

This was not an easy question to answer. 'He re-enacts historical battles,' I said.

Last autumn Billy escaped from the State Hospital and went ambling along the old Indian trails down to the Mason Dixon Line where Civil War era ghosts, in various states of entropy, are hanging around the old battlefields. They mingle with the wild deer population that get culled every season. Over two hundred men gathered together but on opposite sides of the battlefield aiming muskets at each other. The South Carolina regiment had spent months applying for a special licence to fire off their cannon until some 'asshole' they told police, dashed into the centre of the fray in a frickin' nightie.

That night Billy hid inside the old clapboard-covered bridge over Conewego Creek, listening to the cold, clear water rushing beneath him. The rafters of the bridge saw Confederate deserters hung and swinging 125 years earlier and now their ghosts were staring wide-eyed at Billy, snoring in a heap on the splinter-planked wood floor. The ghosts couldn't register why Billy dressed in what looked like a shroud, but they could see his breath made circles in the chilly, night air, where their exhalations could not.

They would have liked to scare the crap out of Billy for the lack of anything better to do in the confines of the covered bridge, now their eternal home but he had sort of fucked with their perception of the mortal realm so they let him be.

My boyfriend's father wasn't interested in my brother which was a good thing, Billy being a kaleidoscope of explanation and all. What he wanted me to see was the photo of Uncle Oscar; Uncle Oscar was wearing a light beige leisure suit and he was looking very perky.

My boyfriend's father wants me to know something about Uncle Oscar. But he has to whisper it into my ear: 'A *fagela*,' he says.

A *fagela* is the pejorative Yiddish term for the more pejoratively translatable term: Faggot. Joy is the name of my boyfriend's mother. Joy is a secretary and Joy dislikes me. I won't know how much until I am seated opposite the guest conductor playing for the Baltimore Symphony Orchestra and his beard. But first the father wants to clarify an important detail about Oscar: 'He's on Joy's side.'

Billy was urinating against the side of a wall of a 7-11 when a kindly man who saw Billy, assumed, dressed as Billy was, he must be part of that morning's baptism and somehow managed to get separated from the flock. The man said he'd give Billy a lift back to the ceremonial waters and Billy, who didn't know what the man was talking about, said he'd appreciate that and if he didn't mind, but could they stop off at the Dairy Queen so Billy could order a DQ Burger, to which the man was only happy to oblige.

My boyfriend's father is called Ivan. We have just leafed through the family attending several peace protest marches and one anti-nuke rally. We are now staring at photos of my boyfriend's sister's wedding: a girl dressed in white lace and jack boots.

The man who found Billy talked about things like ballpoint pens. He told Billy he was a ballpoint pen salesman. 'My clients are mostly car dealerships and insurance,' said the kindly man. 'We do all colours, styles and script... you can have fancy, plain or block,' said the man. Billy politely listened to the man who seemed to know an awful lot about pens. He talked about the spring-loaded vs cartridge and the advantages and disadvantages of both.

'We're branching out into mechanical pencils in the new year.' Then he offered Billy some pens from his glovebox.

'Go on, son,' he said leaning across Billy to flip it open, 'help yourself. You can never have enough writing implements.'

My boyfriend likes to talk about masturbation as though it's something that was just invented. He goes on and on about the glories of masturbation. He talks about masturbation like it's some kind of rare and beautiful moth.

Eventually the blacktop road gave way to a dirt track lined with thickened shrub and tree life; it led to a clearing with a few cars. Where the land dipped down, a clutch of men, women, and little kids, stood up to their knees in the Conowego Creek. The less devout were sitting on the bumper of the cars eating corn chips.

We are all Jews here, in my boyfriend's house. And this is the beginning and the end of what I have in common with these people. My boyfriend is the great *artiste* dressed in black, from his neo-creepy libertine family with no money but lots of social conscience. The direct antithesis of my family: lots of money and absolutely no social conscience. I know what I'm dealing with here. But first I have to concentrate on the sister, and her wedding party is walking all over the sidewalk just outside, the one Joy is going to ask me to shovel ten foot of snow from tomorrow. My boyfriend's father flips through the smiling strangers doing wedding-like things until he reaches the last image.

'Is this a picture, or *what*?' he says.

The kindly man led Billy by the arm to the line of souls waiting to get dunked. The dunker was a thick-set bull of a man wearing army fatigues. He had a black snaggley beard and large aviator-frame sunglasses. He wore a red tank top. He didn't look like the head of a church congregation – more like somebody who hunts deer out of season and only became a preacher as an afterthought.

'You gonna be saved today in this here blessed old creek that flows right into the bosom of Jesus,' said the preacher.

I am staring at the photo of the bride sitting on the groom's lap. He is wearing a top hat and that's it. Her dress is pulled down to her navel. Her breasts are pert like Uncle Oscar.

'Halleluyah!' said the congregants.

'You gonna be admitted into the Kingdom of Heaven,' said the preacher.

'Halleluyah!!' sang the people.

'I am a bar of soap. *The soap of the Lord Almighty.* The soap the angels use to wax clean the floors of heaven and with this holy water in this old creek I will mix the holy soap and the holy blessed water to form holy bubbles to cleanse the abberated and the afflicted, wash their mouths out, wash their souls out, wash their minds out, hang all their sins on the line of God to dry.'

'AMEN,' said the people.

'Are you ready to accept HIM?' The preacher asked each congregant before pushing them backwards into the beautiful water of the creek. 'Are you ready to accept JESUS?' He held them down while they thought about it.

'Yes!!' shouted the people.

They all came up spluttering.

When it was Billy's turn to get dunked he didn't look like anybody else even though he was dressed more appropriately for a baptism than the guy in front of him who wore Bermuda shorts. Billy's gown hung in filthy loops and shreds – he looked like a person who had just escaped from a mental facility – even though technically he was, while the preacher had him by the neck beneath the surface of the creek, looking for Jesus. When at last he released his grip, Billy came back up clutching a 13-inch largemouth bass.

I am trying to focus on Ivan talking about how *grateful* he is that his son is not a dentist. He is saying something like, 'anybody can stick a rubber glove in somebody's mouth and scrape off plaque.'

Isn't that so, Joy?' he yells out from the dining room table to the kitchen.

Joy is washing the dishes. I have politely asked Joy fifty times if she'd like help with the dishes and she has categorically said every single time: 'No, you just sit there.'

Billy managed to walk home, his gown all a flutter, a crazy kite blowing. He'd been to Jerusalem. That's what he told our parents when he rang the doorbell.

The doorbell rings here. Joy is suddenly alive when she sees her. Like a polluted river flowing clean and clear again. Her exuberance over this round-shouldered girl, covered in a tangle of seaweed-like hair and oily skin, I suddenly realise, is proportionate to her dislike for me: the otherwise sullen, passive-aggressive mother who does whatever her husband demands, probably includes beating his bare ass with a hairbrush, is suddenly as animated and excited as Bo Bo the Clown. Joy waves me down the table.

'Let Cynthia sit here,' she says, pointing to my seat. Cynthia lives next door. Cynthia has had a crush on my boyfriend since the second grade. Cynthia mumbles something unintelligible and Joy is beaming. She is unscrupulous this mother, she really is. I relinquish my chair and move next to the father, and this worries me. Not just because I am afraid he will try to stab me, but even worse, he keeps giving me trick questions so I look like a moron. This he will use to his advantage later. The conversation will go something like this:

'Didn't you like her, Dad?'

'Hated her, son.'

'Mom?'

'Hated her more than your father.'

'But, why?' asks my boyfriend.

'Too friendly,' says Ivan, 'we don't like people who try too hard. Plus she believed me when I told her rap dancers get their heads stuck beneath their collarbones.'

'The jam she brought was too expensive,' spat the mother, 'and the little pastries! So fancy! Wrapped in tissue paper with a silver bow. I would have preferred a can of paint.'

'Is she a real blonde?' asks the father, who would wink here because he is a dirty old bastard.

'Does she beat your behind with her boar's bristle brush? The way you like it?' calmly asks Joy.

'If she has sexual hang-ups, well, that's no good,' says Ivan.

'And she told me she preferred Camus to Sartre, Joy. Did you know that son? Camus to Sartre!'

'She's not good enough for our artistic baby,' coos Joy.

'Your mother is right. What are you thinking with, your dick? Use your head, boy, your head!'

FOUL SHOT

Billy got released from the State Hospital ten days ago. It's June 1979 and he's been put on an anti-psychotic medication which is supposed to re-cycle and disperse his incoherent thinking. Otherwise the general is lurking in the basement of our house and following Billy to the toilet. I wonder what the anti-psychotic medication is really supposed to be doing. I know it's making Billy fatter. I know it's making him thirsty. He walks around everywhere with an army canteen filled with tap water strapped to his belt. So far not much else, although Billy's been catching up on his reading – magazines and journals with titles like: *Crime Detective*; *Crime Does Not Pay*; *Criminals on the Run*; *Guns against Gangsters*; and *Mr. District Attorney*. And sometimes he plays basketball with the locals: gang members who play street basketball. They don't care if Billy thinks he's a duck hunter from the outer circle of hell; he plays pretty good basketball for a white boy. The District Attorney knows them too, because their lives tend to revolve around the justice system of southeastern, Pennsylvania. The people who play street basketball have names like Frets, Treazure, and Junks. They play on a cracked tarmac court surrounded by a strong chainlink fence, reminiscent of Barnard County prison. Sometimes they all sit on the tarmac and drink from a pint bottle of Old Crow. Billy isn't supposed to drink anything stronger than water on his new anti-psychotic medication. He isn't supposed to smoke weed. He drinks and smokes anyway and then tells the gang members UFOs are on the loose and probably eating human flesh. They laugh, the gang members. They think this is fanciful crazy-ass honky chatter.

'How come they don't ever snatch a brother?' asked one of the gang members.

'They do,' said Billy – 'it's called Affirmative Action.'

The gang members laughed even harder.

The Assistant DA got in touch with Billy last week, because our mothers play bridge together. He explained his office had their annual basketball playoff between offices – the state attorney's office – and one of the private law firms, and the state team was short a player.

'I'll play,' said Billy.

'Actually, we're short two players,' said the Assistant DA.

Billy said not to worry, he knew somebody.

The following Thursday Billy turned up with Frets – All six foot five of him, and a head shaped like Easter Island. He'd recently been released from prison for assault with a deadly weapon. He had been convicted for throwing a brick at a dental hygienist.

The judge said, 'Guilty'.

Frets raised his hand anyway, like he was in school.

'Yo. Yo. Yo. My Honour,' he said. 'That ain't exactly the way it happened.'

'Oh?' asked the judge, 'then what happened – *exactly?*'

'I threw the brick,' said Frets, 'but the bitch jumped in the way.'

The gavel came down hard and Frets got three and a half years.

The Assistant DA and his team were seated on the bleachers when Billy introduced Frets:

'Yo, man.'

'Brother – hey.'

'Wassup?'

But when the Assistant DA and Frets shook hands, their respective thoughts went like this:

Frets: 'I know this honky from somewhere, but where – *prison*?'

The Assistant DA: 'Uh oh.'

Then the buzzer sounded and rubber soles streaked across the polished wood floor. The ball dribbled and passed and smacked around hard. The private law firm couldn't keep up with the spins, plays, and graceful ease with which the Assistant DA and his team of lawyers, Billy, and an ex-con could control the ball.

When Frets took a foul shot, he stood with one hand on his ass and the other curved around the hard-skinned orange ball, and it slipped through the net like the sun setting. At half-time they drank Gatorade and Frets sat at one end of the bench and the Assistant DA made sure he sat at the other; but Frets kept staring at him anyway.

The Assistant DA's team won: 102 to 88.

In the locker room someone suggested they get pizza to celebrate. The Assistant DA made some excuse about an early morning deposition.

One of his colleagues called him on it. He said, 'The pizza and beer's on the state.'

'He's looking forward to the pizza,' said Billy motioning to Frets. 'Besides, he'll think you don't like him.'

Unfortunately for the Assistant DA, who tried to finagle a seat in Mr Pappy's Pizza Parlor as far away from the giant black man as he could, Frets made sure he sat right opposite.

Frets was the only one indoors wearing sunglasses. He wore his cap backwards. Around his thick bullish neck a huge gold chain was slung, it spelt out: **C-O-O-K-I-E**.

'Is that your girlfriend's name?' one of the senior partners asked him.

'No, man. I like cookies.' Frets drummed his fingers on the tabletop. He puckered his lips. He scratched the side of his cement-like cheeks. He glared hard at the Assistant DA and the Assistant DA couldn't help but notice.

'You like pepperoni?' the Assistant DA asked Frets.

'I ain't got no problem with pepperoni.'

The Assistant DA said he didn't have a problem with pepperoni either.

'Don't I know you from somewhere, man?' He narrowed his eyes, Frets. He tried to look thoughtful rather than threatening but he really did look threatening.

The Assistant DA took a long sip of the pale amber beer from his frosty beer mug. He swallowed it. 'And where might that be from?' he asked.

Frets didn't say another word. He stood up and motioned with an index finger for Billy to follow him, which Billy was happy to do and all, trailing behind the hulk of a human being to a backroom with a pool table. Then he lifted Billy by his collar two-feet off the floor so they could discuss the situation, man to man.

'I'm fine, thank you,' said Billy – 'and you?'

'Why didn't you tell me my man was the DA?' asked a highly irate Frets. He shook Billy until all of Billy's teeth shook back.

Billy wasn't afraid though.

He was tired.

When people get tired sometimes all they want is to go to sleep and not wake up for about two years.

MRS BILLY SYCAMORE

Two years later in the spring of 1981 Billy got married. It was as strange and sudden and miraculous as watching a man get beamed up into a spaceship. When Billy got married there was no wedding. But that didn't matter. He got married.

'What's her name,' I asked our mother.

'Dawn.'

'Not such a great name,' I said.

'No, not so great,' said our mother.

'What does she look like?' I asked.

'Tall.'

'Does she work?'

'In computers,' said our mother.

'Doing what?' I asked.

'Computers,' she said.

'Why does she want Billy?' I asked.

'God knows,' said our mother, 'but thank heaven she does, so be nice to her.'

Dawn was tall. She had big hands and feet. Her hair was brown, lanky and in her face a lot and she wore big eyeglasses.

She was a great sister-in-law for about the two times I laid eyes on her. The first time was in my mother's kitchen at the beginning of the summer. She was studying the fridge magnets.

The second time I met my brother's wife was at the end of the summer, and also the last time. I knew this whole marriage business was too good to be true. She'd been cheating on Billy with a quadriplegic.

If Billy cared he didn't show it. He moved out of their apartment and back to the halfway house.

Then he walked down to the river to go fishing.

THE ENCYCLOPEDIA OF BASKETBALL

The great white house with dark green shutters had a view of the cold-hearted but miraculous river. It sat on five hundred acres of windswept land in the state. There was a pine forest, beech, apple, and willow trees.

The house was owned by the family of my new boyfriend who enjoyed crapping on an open page of the *New York Times* in front me.

He would squat over the paper, much like our dog Marvin.

This new boyfriend knew an awful lot about basketball and when he wasn't crapping on a piece of newspaper, he read *The Encyclopedia of Basketball* on the john. Then he'd ask me to drag up a chair alongside, take the book, and quiz him.

The boyfriend's father, an arrogant old banker with a fine head of hair, used to ask me: 'What are you up to?' as if to imply I was doing something I shouldn't have in a moment when I was doing something I should have, like looking for swallows in the eaves of an old barn falling apart on their property.

I would have much preferred if he asked his own son this question, and the son could reply: 'Nothing much. Just shitting on the Sports' Section of *The Times* and you? How's Mom?'

I wondered how people like my brother were often locked-up and ones like this boyfriend were able to walk around loose in society.

But he never thought like that, my boyfriend. Instead, he'd walk around his apartment and repeat over and over in a fake southern voice: 'You kin fuck my daughters, just keep away from my hogs.'

AMERICAN OPTIMISM

By early May Billy had left the halfway house. He simply walked out of the door and kept going. He walked from the Susquehanna River to the Potomac River in Washington DC. He turned westward like an old pioneer sleeping in the great forests of the pasts, scrambling over farmers' barbed-wire fences and makeshift stone walls from the Civil War. He took the Great Warrior Path past Conoy Creek and Pequea Creek, until Havre De Grace. He saw humpback turtles and naked women like birds fluttering all around him.

By the time he had run out of money he turned back. But first he stole a Camero. Then he took it to a car wash. It was a no-frills car wash. The owners were brothers. Immigrants from Columbia. They were always changing the colour of the place. One day it was canary yellow, and then burnt red, next a medley of pastel shades. Nobody knew if the brothers were bored or had friends who owned a paint store.

Billy drove the Camero straight through the wall of the car wash. Nobody could remember the colour it was that day. The brothers were jumping around the car shouting, fists clenched at Billy, whose head was a bit limp on the steering wheel. He might have been dead on impact. But the brothers didn't mind; they threatened to sue him anyway. It is scenes like this that give the mistaken impression anything is possible in America.

By the time the police arrived Billy had apologised and gave the brothers twenty dollars and our home telephone number and the police gave Billy free accommodation in prison.

The room wasn't very good. Somebody kicked him in his crotch. Somebody else hit him over the head. He sat in a corner on the cold, cement floor and wept because he could still see the moon exploding and nobody would listen. Nobody wanted to see.

It is hard to see sometimes.

PART II

SOUTH OF
THE MASON DIXON LINE

GONE FISHING

It's the first Saturday in June 1981 and I am sitting in the southern Chester County's sheriff's office trying to convince the Sheriff – who drives around with a NO ABORTION sign in the window of his Dodge Dart – that Billy wasn't in his right mind when he drove through the brick wall of the car wash.

I'm watching the Sheriff pick sunflower seeds out of his teeth.

The Sheriff appears to be only half-awake. His feet are crossed on top of a large metal desk that stands like a guard dog between us.

'My mom said we are to pay for all damages and bond money.' I placed the cheque book on the sheriff's desk.

The Sheriff got a big kick out of this. He laughed so hard I thought he'd fall backwards and land in the standing fan pushing the humid air around in languid, dusty circles behind him.

'Your brother, Miss Sycamore, broke into Rhino Haven, mounted a rhino and rode it around like a horse.'

He was waiting for me to say something. I didn't say anything except, 'Oh, OK,' to which the Sheriff interrupted.

'Well, NO, and it ain't "O-*kay*" nor is it how we do things around here.'

I tried to speak but he put his big flat hand up to stop me.

'It's not all the incarcerated had perpetrated – after the night security guard caught him on the animal and shouted at him to git the fig off, the incarcerated took the opportunity thus, to encroach the monkey area where he managed to finagle a cage open, allowing the monkeys free rein.' The Sheriff removed his feet from the desk, leaning so far back in his

147

creaking oakwood swivel chair, with his hands clasped behind his head, that I waited for him to flip out backwards through the open window behind him.

'We got calls from residents in south Chester who thought they was hallucinatin' in the morning when they looked out their window and saw a monkey sitting on the back of a horse.'

Billy did not want any more electroshock therapy. The psycho-ward at the state hospital painted iodine on the sides of his skull and surged enough electricity through his veins to blow-out our whole neighbourhood on Canton Street. I could understand this. I tried to explain to the Sheriff, Billy was not a threat to law and order – even though he tried to kill himself in the car wash; and he did steal the Camaro at the I-Hop in Havre de Grace; and wreak havoc at Rhino Haven – it wasn't like the lunatic who'd been in the papers lately, running around cutting dogs and cats into bite-sized chunks.

I pointed this out to the Sheriff, who had neither interest nor patience, he said, for 'criminal comparisons an' *contrastments*'. He was a pragmatist, a pro-lifer, and he felt obliged to remove the jar on the shelf above the window behind him.

'See this?' he asked. He smacked the jar on the metal desk and shoved it towards me.

'Yes,' I said. 'It's a jar of something.'

'Not just any jar of something – this is the unidentified remains of a human.'

It was a quart jar that once held pickles, peaches, or mayonnaise.

'One day I'm gonna find the person who did this. They chopped off both hands – lookie here...' he said. This is where he pointed to the bones but it didn't look like anything to me but a nightmare stuck in a jar.

'You ever met a murderer?'

'It's funny you should ask that,' I said.

'There is nothing funny about death, young lady, particularly with blunt force trauma and close-range gunshot to the skull.'

'Is that how they died?' I asked. I eyed the jar when I spoke about the person as if they were part of the discussion and could participate in a strange, eternal sort of way.

'It was,' he said. 'But it got worse before the end.' He turned the jar upside down and the forehead tapped the glass.

I didn't want to know how much worse things got for that person. I felt bad enough about the dogs and cats.

'About Billy Sycamore,' I said, wanting to change the subject. But this is when he held up a hand, for silence.

'Billy Sycamore owes Chester County 1000 hours of community service,' said the Sheriff, holding the jar of bones in his hand and turning it over like it was a set of car keys – 'or he can rot in jail until next spring.'

THE TRIPLE D TRAILER COURT

The following Monday Billy got transferred to the Triple D Trailer Court. The front of the double trailer sat in Pennsylvania, the back half in Delaware; and the small patch of yard overlooked Maryland. Billy had never lived in a mobile home. The Sheriff said he'd had the trailer recently fumigated, although he didn't say for what sort of insects exactly, he left that detail kind of open-ended. Billy is to live here for the duration of his parole – while picking dead leaves and trash out of the local cemetery.

The Sheriff pointed out Billy could rent on the Pennsylvania side of the wedge, or pay less in Delaware – but being everywhere, and nowhere all at the same time, it didn't matter one iota because the Sheriff owned the trailer. He also owned the one next door with the fancy flower bed. He had a real racket going, this guy, and the Susquehanna River flowed into the Chesapeake and our river was no more. It became a filtered-down version of fresh water diminished into a network of lesser marshy creeks and streams. Billy had to live here and self-adjust, a highly prized ability among the inflexible of this world: *The self-adjuster.* If left alone Billy might swallow a tube of toothpaste or try to hang himself on his neighbour's clothesline. That's what our mother said. She told me I had to re-adjust my own life to make sure Billy was alright with his; that I had to give up my apartment and my job and my friends all because I wasn't crazy.

'Why can't Dad go?' I asked.

'Your father has a job.' Our father's brain regenerated and he was back at the hospital.

'I have a job,' I said.

'Alice, *please*, this is what families *do*. Nobody else will ever *do* for you what your own family does for you.'

'Then why aren't you going down there?'

And this is where she blew a gasket. 'How could you possibly ask me that? I have too much to do.'

FUNNY LOOKING FIDDLER CRABS

Billy called it a river because if it was a river the man living there wouldn't have minded at all. He would have adjusted himself. It was the kind of person he was: *a self-adjuster*. He lived in a little shack along a tiny, salty inlet that Billy liked to call a river. He lived there with his girlfriend. The girlfriend had white teeth and black skin. Her head wound in colourful rags. The colourful rags became a turban, a skyscraper on her head. She bent low and the building touched the sea foam rushing towards her. She bent low to catch the little pink-faced fiddler crabs that scuttled over rocks. She put the crabs in a hessian sack. But first she peed on the little fiddlers. The crabs hung around in patches, along the rock and sand that was her toilet: a beautiful open-air facility with marine life. She gathered her cotton skirt in her arms, squatted low over the fiddler crab population, and peed on them. Their tiny black eyes blinked and they waved the end of their long antennae stalks. They were funny-looking fiddler crabs too, and busy. They kept busy racing all over wet sand trying to hide from the girlfriend, squeezing in sideways, those crabs did, between rocks. She plucked as many as she could into the darkness of her sack. I liked her. I didn't think she was from around here, though. I know she didn't wear underwear. She pulled up her old long cotton skirt for the whole wide world to see, and then she pissed all over the marine life.

'The water is blue and dark,' she said. She didn't say a whole lot, not what I'd call a big talker, but she did say that.

Billy asked her if there were snakes in the stream. 'The snakes are a problem,' she said, 'but not always, things aren't always so.'

The girlfriend lived beautiful and free by the shack near the salty inlet Billy liked to call a river. They lived together in the shack. Inside it smelt like salt and dried fish and marijuana. A single iron bed pulled up close to one wall. A mix of old lightweight cotton sheets brightened the steel-frame little bed. There was one pillow for two heads. Outside a pile of driftwood. He is a piece of driftwood, her man. His hair, like so many strands of pearl beads, reached his waist bleached by the strong West Indian sunlight from where he came: bleached skin, bleached hair, black calcite eyes, like the night-time sky. He wore little round wire glasses too. Pushed up no-nonsense against his nose, he squinted through them and he faced the water on an old wooden chair, blowing smoke rings from a rolled-up fat stick of dope, he gazed upon the world through his pair of glasses. He blinked his eyes, like a fiddler crab, focusing on the river foam and the horizon beyond, and a rust-coloured sun, disappearing.

'What do you need to wear those glasses for?' I asked him when Billy brought me to meet his new pals. 'They don't have any glass in them.'

All this time the man whittled down a large piece of driftwood into the shape of a pelican. I thought about our grandfather who lived along the Schuylkill River. He loved pelicans. They were his favourite bird. He talked about pelicans like they were personal friends of his. I thought about our overbearing grandmother with the black man's eye. Our grandmother could also be described as a raging Viking, well-hated, except by her husband, a gentle man who liked the pelicans. Then it happened. Like some sort of divine punishment for all of her atrocious acts of mental sadism, our grandmother's eyesight turned against her. It was a slow, degenerative disorder that moved onto the extreme necessity of a corneal eye transplant. The search was on to find a suitable cornea and God bless the Eye Bank of America for matching her up with a black man's cornea from Baltimore. 'I will not have a black man's cornea,' she said.

'Don't be ridiculous,' said our grandfather.

'I won't have it.'

'It is a gift,' he said.

'I won't see things the same.'

'How will you see?' he asked.

'I will see everything the way a black man sees,' she said.

Eventually she had the operation. But only because he said it was not the black man's cornea from Baltimore but a white woman's cornea from Detroit.

'You don't have any glass in your glasses,' I repeated watching him squint. Tall and thin with his waist-length dreadlocks, a good-looking Rastafarian Jamaican, he leaned back on his old chair against the corrugated iron of his hut. His knees akimbo, on his feet a pair of old deck shoes.

'I can't see without them,' he said, and I had to think about this one for a moment.

'But it's a mystery,' I said.

'No,' he said, 'it is no mystery.'

'But it's problematic,' I said.

'It is not problematic.'

'What can't you see?' I asked him.

'The whole world,' he said, 'it's all twisted-up.'

'What's all twisted-up?' I asked.

'The truth,' he said. 'If there's glass in my glasses, it would keep me from seeing the truth.' He paused for a moment to look at the truth, through his glasses. He pushed them against his eyes, bent his head into the dying light of the day, and he squinted for a moment to adjust his vision. 'If you look for the truth you will never be sorry,' he said.

Billy nodded.

Then the man whittled his piece of wood into the shape of a pelican and it flew away.

A GLIMPSE OF SOMETHING
FAR BIGGER (PART ONE)

'So, what brings ya'll down here?'

I encountered her by the row of mailboxes nailed to a horizontal plank of rotting pine. I could say I'm just visiting with my deranged brother on parole.

'My brother is employed by south Chester County.' I try to sound proud.

'Doin' what?' she asks.

'Picking up trash.'

She thinks about this for the time it takes to rip the silver ring off a can of Schlitz.

'That's a good job. Low stress, outdoors.' She chugs down about half the can.

She says if there are any openings to let her know. She wipes her jaw with her elbow. 'What church ya'all belong to?' she asks.

'Church?'

Her name is Mary Eileen and she says she belongs to The Church of God By Faith Incorporated. I have no idea what that means but it means something to Mary Eileen.

'I joined when my soul was saved in public.'

'Was it?'

'At the Baskin 'N Robbins in Cleota.'

'Really?'

'Yup – I saw the Lord's face looking back at me from every flavour of ice cream an' that's when I knew I was being called up.'

'You had the call yet?'

I thought about Mrs Kelman. 'I'm not sure it qualifies,' I said, 'But I believe my brother has.'

Mary Eileen looked pleased.

By the Susquehanna River only Opal Pike thought about Jesus all the time.

We looked for Indian arrowheads in forests filled with pine trees and evergreens, which grew little red berries we chewed and spat out. People said, 'Don't eat those berries, they're poisonous, you'll die.'

We ate them anyway.

A GLIMPSE OF SOMETHING FAR BIGGER (PART TWO)

Billy saw God by the Susquehanna River.

There were a lot of lights, and sharp blasts with a horn. The light dropped to earth in front of him, he said, like a great pane of glass exploding, and it was all because the Kelman's had run over his foot in their four-door Honda Accord.

He was standing by the back door on the driver's side as he watched through the rear window, Mr Kelman put the car in first gear and moved it ever so slightly forward, instead of doing what he should have been doing which was to unlock the door so that Billy could help put their shopping in the car and they could go home from Food Land's parking lot where he had bumped into them – but no – Mr Kelman rolled the car forward just enough until the back wheel landed on top of Billy's right foot and stalled there.

Dear old Mrs Kelman, a woman on a lifetime of large dog breeds, and whom many consider to be dull, if not even a little slow, although she is actually as sly as a buzzard, was smiling at Billy from across the roof of the car. 'So, how's it feel to be out of the mental hospital?' she asked.

Billy said, 'Mrs Kelman, the car is on my foot.' The answer to her question was unsatisfactory, and so she repeated, 'Do you take special medication, Billy?' And he said, 'You wouldn't believe it, Mrs Kelman, but your car is on my foot.' He said it this time with urgency, as perhaps he has been misjudging her all these years, this neighbour with the Great Dane who bit my face for no reason at all, who God help her, apparently was also stone deaf.

'It's quite spectacular how things slow down when you have a car on your foot,' said Billy.

'How, so?' I asked.

'I could see right into the back of Mrs Kelman's throat when she started to shout at Mr Kelman. Nobody said anything relevant like: 'Would you like to stop at the hospital and have an X-ray?' Or 'How's your foot? Do you think you'll ever walk again without the use of a cane?'

'So what did she say.' I asked.

'She talked about her daughter's sixth marriage or something,' said Billy.

I hope this one takes, she said.

OLD SPARKY

After we bonded over heaven Mary Eileen invited me to sit outside her trailer. On white plastic lawn chairs. We are drinking malt liquor out of cans under her RV awning while watching a colour TV she's dragged outside to catch the NASCAR races before an electrical storm blowing in is about to strike us both down dead. Mary Eileen's got on lime green shorts that reach to the top of her slightly chubby knees.

'Have you ever been struck by lightning?' She pauses for a moment to consider my question because perhaps she has been struck by lightning but she was unconscious and could not recall.

'No,' she says, 'I never been struck by lightning but I have been hit by a truck.'

I like Mary Eileen. She told me she once scrubbed all the bathroom tiles in her ex-husband's house while he and his new girlfriend had sex in the lounge. Mary Eileen is both tolerant and tidy.

I wonder what Mary Eileen and I have in common. So far not too much, but this does not always matter in the great scheme of friendship. She told me her ex-husband used to hit her with an aardvark. She could not live with such a man. He hit her with an aardvark and he gave her crabs. She could not stay with such a man. 'I had crabs once,' she said.

'Did you?'

'Yes.'

'What did they look like?'

'Like head lice but in the wrong direction.'

'Where'd you catch them?'

'From a toilet seat.'

'I thought you caught them from your ex-husband?'

'No. We were happy then. I caught them from a toilet seat.'

'But you can't catch crabs from a toilet seat.'

She is indignant here. 'I did catch crabs from a toilet seat.'

I am silent.

'Have you ever had crabs?' she asks.

'No.'

'Well, then, how would you know?'

'But I have had head lice. And fleas,' I say.

'From a cat?'

'No. A monkey, a monkey on Second Street gave me fleas,' I said, thinking about Chester whom nobody remembered to rescue when the flood poured into the basement of the Prom Queen's house and he drowned.

I notice Mary Eileen looks nothing like her aunt. Mary Eileen is short, dark and stumpy while her aunt is tall, slim, blonde, and wears bright red slacks and yellow high heels. She walks to the mailbox and puts things in there and takes things out. She loves fast cars and the Miami Dolphins. But I do not know what she is up to in her mailbox. When she's not in her mailbox, Mary Eileen's aunt seems to spend a lot of time in hairdo maintenance. Hers is a buoyant and elaborate tangle shaped like the state capitol dome.

'What are you doing today, Mary Eileen?' I ask.

'Going to church,' she says. 'It's Tuesday.'

I really like Mary Eileen. Above her upper lip grows the shadow of a moustache which she refuses to bleach or wax. She is her own person, this girl.

'Where's your ex-husband these days?' I ask.

'Out hunting,' she says.

'What's he hunting?'

'Hog,' she says, 'he's out hunting hog.'

'Around here?'

'No, in Florida.'

Mary Eileen said she used to live along the Caloosahatchee River, by the tidal stones and roots of the dark salty waters flowing, but she said her circumstances changed, as circumstances tend to do, thanks to her ex-husband, who Mary Eileen graciously referred to as 'kinda' violent and 'sorta' cheating, so she moved up north, and into her Aunt Vine's (Delvine) trailer next door. It was supposed to be for a few weeks but it's become a good eighteen months 'give or take'.

'We went hog hunting on our honeymoon though,' said Mary Eileen. 'It was real nice.'

I try to picture Mary Eileen dressed in camouflage fatigues chasing after a hog with a loaded .22. It's surprisingly easy.

'What do you do with a dead hog?' I ask.

'During the Super Bowl we'd eat a lot of spare ribs,' she said.

We don't have any hogs by the river. Not running around wild anyway, as far as I know. We've got rabbits, wood chucks, and deer. There are black bears that break into people's homes. We've got people who dress up in period clothes, take a musket, and kill things in the woods. We've got teenagers with BB guns who shoot a squirrel in the ass and think it's hilarious. Then they get drunk and die in a car accident five years later.

'They still got the electric chair in Florida,' says Mary Eileen – 'Old Sparky?'

I don't know Old Sparky. I don't know much about anything. I know even less about hogs, yet I don't ask Mary Eileen what she thinks of Old Sparky. However her Aunt, who has already been to the mailbox ten times today, the aging beauty queen, tall, feminine, and birdlike comes out with: 'Fry them.'

The earth is absorbing the summer thunderstorm of the day and the river is churned, full of silt and minerals floating to the Chesapeake in one direction and the Atlantic, beyond. There can be a hot wind blowing across the river, or not. But I don't wait around to watch the sun fall. I don't see the small barges and little tugboats coming into Havre de Grace, but it doesn't mean they aren't there – just because I can't see them, they exist somewhere, for somebody. Instead I stand around and wait for lightning to strike my head. I cannot defy my own feelings. You can defy them for just so long and then you have to get out of your armchair and do something. This is when I lean next to a metal pole and wait for lightning to strike. Or nothing to strike, at all.

SUMMER RAIN

All that summer Billy had a lot of insect visitors.

It started with a caterpillar. It had a horn protruding from its behind and it sat on top of the tin garbage can waiting for something. The individual who rented the mobile home directly on the other side of my brother, and closer to Delaware, stood next to me one humid mid-July day, observing the creature. He wore red suspenders over white T-shirts, the man: short, bald, fat, fifty-five and his name was Eugene Strout. I called him Mr Strout and the first thing he said to me was, 'Call me Gene.'

'Okay, Mr Strout,' I said. Mr Strout was the Sheriff's brother-in-law and the trailer park's maintenance personnel.

'Now that critter has a mean old bite,' he said referring to the caterpillar. 'It's called a Puss.'

'A Puss?' I asked.

'That's correct,' he said with a wink.

Mr Strout liked talking about the Puss Caterpillar. I wasn't sure I liked him talking about it, because he seemed to like talking about it a little too much. It was the same way I felt when he installed a new oven in Billy's trailer last month. After he explained the self-cleaning mechanism to me, with the understanding I would relay this information to my brother, who only cooked frozen pizza and fish fingers in there and not elaborate suppers or cakes like Mary Eileen and her aunt, he grabbed hold of my arm, lowered his voice and said, 'I did this… for *you*.'

Well I thought, 'Oh Christ,' but I didn't say that. I said, 'Thanks, Mr Strout.'

He said, 'Call me Gene.'

Billy seemed to be surrounded down here: He had the

ubiquitous Eugene Strout, and on the other side, the nun-like and exquisite emotional and psychic simplicity of Mary Eileen and her capital punishment aunt. Opposite, over the road in Maryland, was a man who had a lot of packages delivered to him in brown paper and white string.

Whenever it rained down here I noticed the insects got all jumpy and came out of their holes. There are different species of ant: the carpenter ant, the black ant or wood ant, the pavement ant, the odorous ant that smells like coconuts when crushed and a sugar ant, a sweet little tea-coloured thing. There were big bugs that flew and dropped their wings like a thousand butterflies then they'd morph into wood-eating termites. There were silverfish and earwigs, the house centipede and killer bees from Texas. There was also the cockroach. The King Pin of all insects: Banded, Brown, Black, American, German. I have chased them with a broom around my brother's trailer. I have chased a particularly clever one up all the fake panelled walls and behind the greasy furniture and under the industrial carpet with bug spray.

There is a woman who writes books about the telepathic link we have with animals. She says the animals we knew in life are waiting for us on the other side. I knew the cockroach I sprayed had things on its mind. I don't know how I knew that, but I knew.

It's raining fish outside and there is a lull in the conversation and I don't like conversational lulls. 'Have you got any cockroaches?' I ask Mr Strout.

'Nope – can't say's we do.'

When I told Mr Strout about the cockroaches running free through the Sheriff's rental trailer he just shrugged. 'You're welcome to call an exterminator,' he said, but translated he meant: 'you're welcome to call an exterminator and you can pay for it.' I know this because this is the same man who got my brother to repair the pump under the toilet tank. Billy used fishing tackle and a paper clip.

The exterminator company dress their employees in bright orange one-piece boiler suits. They wrap entire mobile homes and single-storey houses in matching orange sheeting, like a piece of contemporary art, and set off fumigation bombs. Then they jump into compact cars and vans fitted with mouse ears and a tail. Mr Strout had his trailer fumigated. I watched the exterminators tumble out of the mouse car with tanks of poison gas strapped to their backs that summer.

Billy decided he'd prefer to handle our roaches on a case by case basis and let the wood ants and termites bore through the plywood, chipboard and pine cladding of the Sheriff's beige and cream-coloured trailer, with all their insect hearts.

Eugene Strout didn't work of course. As the Triple D Mobile Home Parks 'Maintenance Engineer' and the Sheriff's brother-in-law, he took for himself (according to Billy who was told by Aunt Vine) a percentage from the rental of the mobile homes, so he could stay at home and build an attached garage. A truck from a local lumber yard rumbled into the trailer park. It dumped stacks of pine timber boards and something like hairy-looking coconut bark onto his pebbled drive. There were galvanised nails and screws stacked in neat little boxes. For days the work dragged on. I couldn't think through the buzz saw and the drill. I was starting to resent Mr Strout and his DIY and I wanted to send Billy's insects over there to have a really good chew.

HEART AND BONES

When fishermen cast their nets on the water they reel in other things, not always fish-related. It's like that when you change rivers. You cast your net and pull towards yourself whatever comes in, perhaps too quickly, in an attempt to feel anchored. You try to be pleasant, be a good neighbour.

The neighbours invited Billy to a Tupperware Party. There were five women – including me and all squeezed on the blue velveteen sofa in Aunt Vine's trailer.

The Tupperware Rep, Gaylene Filbert-Butz, was tough-talking and pleasant as hell, and she truly believed in the virtues of her product. Billy seemed to particularly enjoy her lecture on bugs.

'You can get into some real problems with flour. How many of you gals – oh and guy,' she winked at Billy – 'do baking?'

Everybody raised their hands, including Billy.

'What do you bake?' I asked him.

'None of your damned business,' he said.

'If you've ever seen little black flecks in your flour,' and Gaylene hesitated here, waiting for somebody to concur, but the women were too smart for that, 'that'll be your grain weevil.'

Gaylene went on like this for a while. She told us flour beetles, meal worms, and grain weevils are not harmful. 'They make the flour look bad, but if you eat them you won't die,' she said. 'And you can even sift them from flour,' she said.

'Okay,' said Gaylene to the group –'who's got moths?'

These ladies weren't going there.

'Meal worms?'

Dead silence.

Then: 'How about cockroaches?'

I raised my hand. 'My brother's got cockroaches,' I told her and all the others glared at Billy although Gaylene looked strangely ecstatic. Her voice lowered to a severe whisper, into the true Tupperware professional she was.

'Are they getting into your flour, honey?' asked Gaylene.

'Actually, they're getting into his dish gloves,' I said.

One afternoon I had pulled on a dish glove in Billy's trailer to wash up some dishes and when the pinky finger of my left hand pressed into something, I made the intellectual connection like this: 'This is no pebble or walnut shell.' It was an eye, or carapace-hard body. The thorax, the bristles on its legs, its antennae touched my flesh, then my conscience. It knew. All curled-up in a ball barely alive, tucked away in my rubber glove waiting.

It was an intelligent, vengeful bug. I had already tried to track it down earlier, gave it one good blast of Bug-B-Gone. It wasn't going to die a straightforward bug death and now I knew this. It had been waiting. And I understood this: All that time between life and death, it was waiting.

And I felt a dark storm coming. I felt it waiting in my heart and bones.

THE BIG HOUSE

The Sheriff had on his khaki trousers and his matching khaki short-sleeved shirt. The gun and holster, handcuffs dangling. I thought for sure he was coming to beat the shit out of Billy for slacking off in the cemetery or not washing the towels and linen at the Geronimo Hotel.

But instead the Sheriff strode right over to announce he was releasing Billy back into the mental health association of the state of Pennsylvania, 'on good and proper recognizance,' he said, because a week earlier Billy had been first to arrive on the scene when Eugene Strout was being ripped to shreds by a bear.

'You done good, son,' said the Sheriff. 'You kin start packing.'

Billy had heard Mr Strout's screams and saw, or what he thought he saw by moonlight in the half-finished garage, a discombobulated bear's head floating in the gloom. Billy reacted by hurtling his front stoop – the two cinderblock bricks – at the bear. Unfortunately one struck Mr Strout in the head; the other bounced off the plyboard walls of the garage which scared the bear into the surrounding darkness of the night, but also whacked Mr Strout on the other side of his head.

The Sheriff yelled over a hello to Aunt Vine who'd been trying to listen to our conversation – she held up a can of Budweiser.

'I'll stick to beer, thank you very much.'

Back home Billy moved into a halfway house by the Walnut Street Bridge. An old truss bridge spanning the length of the Susquehanna River. Billy called it the 'Big House'.

The halfway house had a pitched roof and dark red brickwork. Dandelions grew along the edge of a perimeter chain-link fence as if they were a proud and important flower. In winter they became twisted stalks and crushed brown leaves.

Billy watched TV in the house. Or he sat outside in a little metal folding chair reading *Three Roads to the Alamo*. He ate gingersnaps in the shape of stars, piglets, and goblins.

'You want the goblin?' I asked one late autumn afternoon during a visit.

'I've got enough goblins,' he said.

Billy hadn't been doing much. He told me he joined a support group to discuss Ingmar Bergman films. He said one of the people in his group was writing an autobiography.

'Why?'

'Because they have nothing better to do.'

Billy said there wasn't much in the book except a single Swedish mother and an old drunk for a stepfather, a communist who never returned library books, a chain smoker who liked to wear the mother's underwear. 'They're having some trouble with the stepfather, though,' said Billy.

'Why?' I asked.

'They're stuck,' he said.

'Stuck how?'

'Stuck as in they don't know what to do with him,' said Billy – 'which is pretty ironic since he's dead and they can do whatever they want with him.'

'Like the Confederate general,' I said. 'Long gone.'

'Yeah,' Billy said, 'Long gone.'

'And he's never coming back,' I said.

'No,' said Billy, 'he's not.'

PART III
THE DELUGE

THE UPSIDE OF MANIA

By October 1981 I was back in New York working for a weekly news magazine in their research department. I found an apartment in the West Village. Billy moved back into his old bedroom on Canton Street. He had been encouraged by some state-funded psychologists to 'brain storm' vocations and he came up with a petting zoo. He would sit at the kitchen table and tell Opal.

'Where you gonna keep these critters?' Opal asked.

'In the garage,' said Billy.

'You can't keep no tiger in the garage! I ain't gonna work here no more,' said Opal.

'No tigers,' said Billy.

'How you gonna pay for all this?'

'My disability cheques.'

Apparently Billy managed to convince a local farmer he'd make a fortune in untapped children's birthday parties and if he lent Billy a tame and friendly chicken, he'd cut the farmer in ten per cent. The farmer, who wore mutton-chop sideburns, a rubber apron, and carried an empty tin pail around – said he would lend Billy the chicken. Billy was ecstatic. He spent two days in a fevered sweat creating flyers which he shoved in people's mailboxes all over Caulderton. Next he waited by the phone. He waited about two weeks, pacing around the house, calling the farmer every single day, sometimes three times a day, to give him a blow by blow of how rich they were going to be.

'After this, we can start a chain of petting zoos throughout the county, then the state, then in the next three states, then tomorrow – the whole world.' He really had the farmer going.

At last somebody called. It was from a family who recently moved to Caulderton from New Delhi. The father was working as an urologist at one of the local hospitals. The petting zoo was for their six-year-old son's birthday party. The family wanted to impress his new American classmates in the second grade.

Billy turned up with one of the farmer's pet chickens, a large salamander Billy had caught in the creek behind our house, a tree frog, and 'Delicious' Opal's son's python (who was getting a five per cent cut) and just as a last, impulsive thought, our dog, Marvin.

The Indian family lived in a two-storey colonial house with powder-blue shutters and aluminum clad siding. They had a neat and tidy flower bed and a doormat that said 'God Bless America'. The family was very happy to be living in America and their little boy overjoyed when Billy pulled up in our mother's white Cadillac with the animals loaded in the front and back seats in wire cages.

It was a beautiful bright early October day and the birthday party was set in the backyard of the Indian family's house. An oil cloth covered an outdoor picnic table. On top sat a glass bowl of fruit punch and a large store-bought sheet cake with white icing which spelled out Happy Birthday Rajit.

To look animal-friendly, Billy wore a pair of farmer overalls over a Hawaiian shirt. He brought out the animals in their cages and lined them up under an oak tree.

'When can we pet them?' asked the birthday boy.

'You can pet the dog all you want,' said Billy. He pointed to Marvin who was watching the hot dogs and hamburgers being cooked on the charcoal bbq. The doctor father was wearing a tall chef's hat and a long white apron. Marvin didn't leave the doctor's side.

'I already have a dog,' said the birthday boy. While Billy and the birthday boy were having a debate, all the other children were crouched down around the salamander's cage. The children were screaming. The salamander had grabbed the frog and only two of the frog's legs were visible now from the salamander's mouth. The Indian mother was very upset and yelling for Billy to 'please do something quickly' so Billy opened the cage, grabbed the frog's legs and the salamander's body then pulled both amphibians in opposite directions. The children appeared a little bit traumatised; all of the girls started to cry. It took Billy about a minute of serious tugging to get them separated, then he put the stunned and saliva-covered frog in with the chicken. One of the children let 'Delicious' out to slither around in the grass. The birthday boy wanted to pet the chicken, and to show off to his new American friends so he grabbed it by the neck and it flapped its terrified wings all crazy and the boy dropped it and the chicken ran but not fast enough as the snake got hold of it and locked its jaws around the chicken's head. Only the feet moved up and down and this time the Indian father came over to hit the snake with a plastic spatula. While the doctor was distracted, Marvin leapt up several times and managed to eat most of the burgers and hot dogs after which he growled and snarled at the mother's sari – as if it was some sort of billowing cat. Then he grabbed the sari, tearing it straight off her head, then proceeded to rip it to shreds.

The Indian family refused to pay Billy his $35 petting zoo birthday party fee. They said if this was the 'American Way' they wanted none of it.

The farmer asked Billy for his ten per cent in addition to a new chicken.

The python, however, returned to Opal's house, fat and replete, having had a wonderful time.

THE DOWNSIDE OF MANIA

The trees by the river are resplendent in green leaves. Heaven sees the old tree branches, leafless and bony, resurrect each spring and absorb the rain and sunlight, flowing through roots like blood in the veins. People can't do that, they think they're so clever, but they can't do that. The leaves however, who say nothing, who ask for nothing, they can.

It's March 1982 and Billy is strapped in a wheelchair, he is asking for a gun. 'Just kill me – can you do this one thing?' He will ask me this when I haven't seen him since last summer and I am introducing him to my new expendable boyfriend.

'This is my boyfriend,' I say. The boyfriend looks nervous. He thrusts his hand out to shake my brother's hand, as if my brother is sitting not in a wheelchair but at the head of a conference table, the CEO of some big and important company.

'How ya doin', says Billy, '…can you bring me a gun?'

It is a bright but windy day at the state mental hospital and we are pushing Billy around the grounds in a wheelchair. The earth is still soaked and damp from snowmelt. It's hard to push Billy around out here.

After the petting zoo Billy tried driveway re-surfacing using only exterior black paint. But in the terrible rains that spring, it simply washed off. Juan Goldstein was home from graduate school where he was doing an MA in philosophy and he told Billy: 'But it looks good. So don't worry.'

But Billy decided he would start a new business, this time the rug shampooing business – just him and the rug cleaning machine which he rented from Mack's Hardware. Billy only had enough disability money to rent the machine for one day a week so when people called he scheduled them all on the same day.

'Tuesday?' they'd say – 'Can you come Wednesday afternoon?'

'Uh, I'll check my book,' Billy would say, then he'd pretend to flip through pages, and he'd make some clicking noises with his tongue, tap a pencil against the phone and finally say – 'I already have jobs those days – but I can squeeze you in Friday.'

This made Billy's Carpet Cleaning business appear busy and professional.

For the first two weeks it was straightforward. Billy would collect the rug shampooer from the hardware store by 7am and load it into the back seat of our mother's white Cadillac. He also used their standard rug shampooing products. Everything was easy until it wasn't, as most things are and Billy had to face a rust-coloured stain on a client's wall-to-wall powder-blue carpet. Billy plugged in the machine and it whirred happily in soapy circles. The stain didn't lift however. Billy re-worked the spot. The stain was still there and it looked darker.

Billy went into the client's kitchen and looked under the sink. He found a product called 'Devil Stain Remover' so he poured this directly onto the spot and went out to have a pastrami sandwich. When Billy got back the stain was gone but in its place was a bleach spot the size and shape of a world map.

The woman called later to scream. She wanted Billy's company insurance to replace the whole 9x12 piece of carpet. But Billy didn't have any insurance. Our parents had to replace the whole carpet. Depressed and dejected Billy drank a six-pack of beer and smoked a few joints on lithium, a specific drug for manic depressives, where they specifically state: don't drink alcohol or take drugs. Billy did both.

He can't walk very well anymore. In fact he can barely talk either. His words spill out like knotted tackle but I can decipher the gun speech, holding two fingers to his skull and saying 'click'. He drops his hands, his shattered green eyes a prism of darkness and he says: 'Then let's go fishing.'

ALL KINDS OF MANIACS

The following summer I came home to visit and bumped into that old Buddha, Mrs Stanley. The first thing she says to me is, 'I heard Billy tried to swallow a tube of toothpaste. Colgate, I believe.'

It is late July and the water level in the river is low this time of year, there's even a sandbar where fishermen can stand mid-river in their green rubber waders and catch bass, practically in their bare hands, in the backwash.

Billy is confined to the isolation ward for trying to swallow the tube of toothpaste. The isolation ward has a heavy metal light-grey door. The walls are white, windowless. There is only a bare mattress on the floor. It could be jail but it isn't, in our little town, where the paddlewheel ferry still crosses the river upstream. We have billionaires and perverts, gun maniacs, religious maniacs, sex maniacs, all kinds of maniacs. This is a normal town, like any other, any place else on this good earth, but the difference is this is my hometown. Nowhere else, no matter how long I will ever occupy space there, can ever be called the same: My Hometown. It is with a strange sort of reverence that I sit along the river now, and think, how did it come to this?

'He used an electrical cord to strangle himself,' said Juan. Juan was used to Billy's revolving door mental breakdowns.

Catfish prefer corn, but bass like fresh bait. In particular, hellgrammites, a primeval-looking insect with a hard black shell and two front pincers. Billy used to catch hellgrammites. He'd find them clinging to rocks along the riverbank. He'd put the fishhook behind the hellgrammite's head and when the bass caught sight of it they'd almost jump straight onto the hook.

The combination of toothpaste and strangulation left Billy looking like a racoon. I barely recognised him. His beautiful blond hair had turned grey overnight. A lot of blood vessels in each green eye had burst from the pressure. He looked like somebody unrecognisable, somebody I never thought I'd ever meet, let alone be related to. His eyes, black, blue, and bloodshot, dangled from his skull; a hanged man that didn't get hung right.

'Maybe you're not meant to die,' I said.

'Maybe I am,' said Billy.

Since the strangulation Billy's voice is hoarse and raspy, but he keeps talking about a man kidnapped by aliens over in Union County. He said all the blood had been drained from the man's body, his anus cut out and his jaw excised. Two circular holes laser-burned into his chest.

'Aliens can be sociopaths too,' said Billy. 'You think sickos are only confined to this planet? And they mutilated him while he was still alive. No Novocain,' said Billy.

'Who tells you this stuff?' I asked him.

'Don't worry,' he says, 'I know people.'

The river makes sounds and noises, it is audible yet indefinable. The sluice over rocks, a delicate breeze through overhanging trees, the water pulses downstream. Some fishermen don't meander too far towards the weir; they are afraid. But some have been close enough to see the weir. Billy's always saying he's going to conquer the weir. 'Why?' I ask.

'Because I can't go upstream,' he says.

HALFWAY BETWEEN THIS WORLD AND THE NEXT

Eventually Billy's eyeballs moved back into their sockets and the bruises healed over time. Only a shadow crossed his face. By late August the mental authority of the state of Pennsylvania placed Billy in another halfway house.

It was an old wooden structure with a sagging front porch overlooking a two-lane road and big glimpse of the river. It was damp all year round and on the porch there were a couple of beat-up chairs and a tin pot catching raindrops from a hole in the eaves. When the roof leaked indoors, Billy sat on the lumpy sofa holding an umbrella over his head. He watched Mannix while it rained on his head.

I'd come down to the halfway house to see Billy. Once on a very hot summer evening, when fireflies lit up the whole world, I arrived in time to find a black man locked inside the closet. 'What's he doing in there?' I asked Billy.

'They say they're going to lynch him,' said Billy.

I looked at Billy's housemates. I knew they had mental problems of every size and shape ever produced. One of them was pounding on the closet door, 'We're coming fer ya, boy,' he said.

'Shouldn't we call someone?' I asked Billy.

'They're only messing around,' my brother said.

I could hear the black man weeping.

'Are you sure?' I asked. He shrugged.

'How should I know,' said Billy. 'They're crazy.'

AN UNREPENTANT DEVIANT

One thing Billy used to say about his hallucinatory mind was: Just because you can't see it doesn't mean it doesn't exist. Like years earlier, on that singular March afternoon in 1970, Joseph Lightfoot was considering the sandbar by the Lincoln Avenue Bridge as an excellent spot for some early evening fishing when a man floated past him downstream. Joseph Lightfoot yelled, 'Ahoy.'

When the man ignored him, he waded into the neck-deep water and let the current carry him until he could catchhold of the collar of the man's ragged-wool grey coat.

'Ahoy,' the Indian repeated.

The man didn't answer. He had a gash on his head and a piece of his left ear was missing. His eyes were shut.

'Are you dead?'

'I don't think so,' said the man.

'You had me there for a moment,' said the Indian.

'I have been accosted,' said the man, 'by a crafty Negro.'

'Is that so?' said the Indian.

'With pale kinkajou hair. An albino one, he was. No bigger than a dwarf. He hit my skull with a rock, shot at me then tossed me into the river like a dead eel,' said the man.

'Why'd he do it?'

'How should I know how a psychotic individual thinks?' said the man.

Joseph Lightfoot said nothing.

'I crawled out of the river, then the sonofabitch tried to shoot me so I had to jump right back in,' said the man.

'You can walk now. It's shallow,' said the Indian.

'I'd prefer to lie on my back if you don't mind,' said the man.

The Indian shrugged and pulled the man by his collar onto shore. Then he helped him over to a fallen tree stump.

'Here,' said Joseph Lightfoot. He gave the man a pint bottle of Firewater.

He took a big, greedy gulp, the man. His eyes went wide as a pie and he looked as if he was about to choke but it passed.

'You from 'round here?' asked the Indian.

'No,' said the man who did not offer his place of origin and the Indian did not ask.

He was sitting on the stump, his head cocked to one side, and his too-short trouser legs rolled up to his kneecaps. He thumped an ear to dislodge some water.

'You need a ride somewhere? My truck's just on the road,' the Indian pointed behind him.

He shook his head. 'I left my car parked on the road. The rapscallion come sniffin' whilst I be enjoyin' a view of the swift-flowing waters of this here fine old river,' said the man. 'Next thing I know I'm in the river. The bastard tried to shoot me and I'm in the water, baptised a second time, and I think I'm going to float to Galilee.' He let out a hacking old cough, that sounded like tuberculosis. 'For a second I thought you be the Devil hisself. But on further perusal I see you just an Injun.'

'Iroquois, actually,' said Joseph Lightfoot.

'I'm not trying to argue pejoratives with you,' said the man.

Joseph Lightfoot had removed a packet of tobacco and some papers from his dark green satchel. He had one foot on a rock while he rolled a smoke and listened to the man.

'I mean no disrespect,' said the man, 'Be you of the Iroquois nation – tis' God doing His Own Mighty will.' The man helped himself to another swig of the home brew. 'Besides I hear the average Injun got a wango the size of the mighty buffalo – although I ain't got the gumption nor the perchance to have gazed upon such a magnificent beast.'

'You know what I think? I think you're one of those unrepentant deviants,' said the Indian striking a match on the rock.

'Hogs' wallop,' said the man. 'It is only for curiosity sake I inquire. Ain't you got curiosities?'

'Hmmm,' said the Indian.

The man began to fan himself with a piece of old newspaper he found lying by his foot.

'You say a dwarf did this?' the Indian asked, pointing at the man's head and ear with his cigarette.

'And a wily one at that,' said the man.

'With a knife-like face and one eye?' asked Joseph Lightfoot.

'Now that you mention it,' said the man.

'Was he two dimensional or three?' asked the Indian.

'I didn't take in no dimensions,' said the man, 'he was a little black one with white hair. Jumped out of the bush at me like a rattler.'

'Know what I reckon?' said the Indian.

'I ain't a mind reader,' he said.

'You're gonna bring me bad luck,' said the Indian, who pulled out a bow and arrow from behind him and aimed it at the man's heart.

The man sprang to his feet like somebody set fire to his backside. But he didn't go towards the river. Instead he ran into the woods. And Joseph Lightfoot laughed so hard all the comets and stars fell into the river.

THE DEATH OF MRS SPRAGUE

They say the flood in June 1972 didn't start with a hurricane in the Bahamas but with the snowmelt on the Blue Ridge Mountains.

Heavy spring rains forced the Susquehanna River's water levels to swell and overflow its banks.

Places normally dry and pleasant became insupportable, inundated, drowned. A cement sculpture became an underwater feature, a park bench, driftwood.

The water turned deadly and dark. It swallowed houses and buildings and people. It turned gravedigger, upending whole cemeteries carrying coffins on its tide along with grand pianos, farm animals, office furniture and Mrs Sprague. Such is the power of water.

She was wrenched free of the telephone pole to which she clung, her life caught between a whirlpool of mud, water, and waves, in the pitch black centre of night, bootless, boatless, shoeless, her raincoat not waterproof, like the saleswoman had promised. She had only gone out to buy cat food.

It is many years after the flood. I have just walked past a man who cannot move or think. His right leg is permanently crossed over his left knee. He is wearing a suit and tie. Nothing fancy. He is reading a newspaper through a pair of metal eyeglasses.

I am watching some youths hold a gun to his temple. They are saying something to the man. It probably says something about me if I think a bunch of black kids holding up an iron sculpture of a white man is funny. Although I am thinking about poor Mrs Sprague now, who drowned like a kipper in a net.

The Indian told Billy: 'Fish can drown too.'

Billy told me it seemed paradoxical enough to make sense, as paradoxical things often do – which is the whole paradox in the first place.

Therefore a drowning fish is perfectly sensible.

CROWNED NIGHT HERONS

I remember I wasn't exactly looking for him, but still, I was walking along the river when I happened to bump into him anyway, tying flies. It was late July 1984. I was in between jobs, having been fired from the magazine, and in between boyfriends. I felt aimless and wandering; sleepless from nightmares and dark, troublesome thoughts.

I noticed the water remained at springtime levels, high, moving fast and mud-coloured. He'd been missing for three days. No word. No call. He looked up at me.

'Hey, Alice,' he said. 'How's New York?'

'Hey,' I said. 'It's alright. Where've you been? Everybody's been worri…'

'I stole a canoe,' he said.

'So give it back,' I said.

'I can't. It's floating somewhere downstream. I used it to go around Jasper Island. I wanted to see the black-crowned night herons.'

'Did you see any?'

'No,' he said, 'so I paddled over to Hawk Island.'

'What's on Hawk Island?'

'Indian land.'

'You shouldn't be messing around there,' I said. Maybe it was the slanting light of the day but Billy looked so pale, almost diaphanous.

'You look well,' I lied. I was just grateful to see him out of that sad old wheelchair.

'You don't know the half,' he said.

'Come home,' I said, 'it's late.'

'I bumped into Joseph Lightfoot on Halfway Island, he scared me half to fucking death,' said Billy.

'What was he doing?'

'Puffing on a pipe.'

'So?'

'So the smoke made dark rings in his ribcage and a lot of mice ran out.'

'That's a crazy story,' I said.

'But a good story,' said Billy.

'Let's go, okay?'

'Okay,' said Billy. 'You go on ahead and I'll catch up.' He was kneeling down, his head over a bucket of fish.

'I'm going to let them go first – go on, Alice.'

'I'll wait till you let them go.'

'Okay,' said Billy. 'But first I've got to take a leak.'

I watched him vanish, slide into the woods, and the whole world stood still until he looked back and said, 'Alice?'

'Yeah?' I shouted back.

'I have to tell you something.'

'What?'

'I'm sorry.'

'Sorry?'

'It wasn't your fault – do you hear me?'

Nuestra vidas son los rios
Que van a dar en el mar

'He would have *killed* you – he had it coming… so leave it now, let the river carry it off.'

que es el morir…

What he said gave me a terrible chill. I swallowed back the fear. My hands shook terribly.

It was starting to get dark and the wind rose up on the river making small waves that rocked the bucket with Billy's fish. I walked towards the edge of the woods but I didn't want to go in after my brother.

'I'm going home now,' I shouted to the woods, so dark, it looked like a solid brick wall. 'Do you hear me? I'm going home.' My voice echoed around the tall pines and only a squirrel stopped to stare at me.

Billy didn't reply but I was sure he'd heard me and I don't know why, but I turned to the bucket with a good-sized brown speckled trout swimming and I walked into the river, just up to my knees. I held the squirming and slippery and beautiful fish just below the surface of the water like a drowning man against the current, and I let it go.

THE POLICE

When I got home I told our parents I saw Billy by the river. Billy was fine. He'd not had an 'episode', he's not trying to walk to Maine in his underwear. He's only fishing but they couldn't hear me. They were sitting around the kitchen table drinking gin.

'The police found a body in the river.'

'Whose body?' I ask. This news terrified me.

'They didn't say but they asked if we'd seen Billy,' said our mother looking frightened of some dark, terrible thing she couldn't yet comprehend.

'Billy used to say he shot a man,' said our dad – 'maybe they found a trace of him.'

Our mother's violet eyes opened wide. I felt hot and icy all at once.

'Are you alright, Alice?' asked our mother.

'Call the lawyer,' said our father.

'Why?' I asked. I didn't recognise my own voice. It sounded shrill, almost hysterical. All those stories about the electric chair: *Sure they fry women too – not as many as men – but they get the volts.* I could hear Aunt Vine's voice ringing through my skull.

Our father cut a lime. Our mother wrung her hands.

I tried to picture him – a Confederate hat, a finger bone, half his ear missing – what we did to him – what could not be helped.

But now the police are here, and I hold my breath. For sure I am going away in handcuffs. But the only body they have come to discuss is my own brother Billy Sycamore's – caught and held down in the weir three days ago. *Three days ago.*

(SOMEWHERE) DOWN
THE CRAZY RIVER

It happened a year earlier, when I was home for Mae Lacey's wedding. It was June 1983 and I was a bridesmaid.

He had managed to coax her with that damn pack of Sugar Babies. She'd left the back door unlocked as usual and he was pissed off as he needn't have bothered with the candy after all. I was in my bedroom at the time, trying on the bridesmaid's dress: rose-coloured taffeta and tea-length when I heard the screams.

I figured she just wanted my attention so I took my sweet old time, which in retrospect I still feel pretty bad about – when all of a sudden I find a total stranger standing in the middle of our lounge trembling with rage. He had Glonell – and this must have hurt like a bastard – by those wiry little braids of hers – I thought her head was going to snap off dandelion-like with the first blast of wind. In the man's other hand I noticed he held a photograph of my brother. The one from the mantelpiece, when Billy was twelve years old, almost thirteen – smiling all freckly and sweet, holding up a big brown trout on the line and I hear the man shouting, 'This little sonofabitch tried to kill me. Blew a hole right through my ear.' This is where the man drops Glonell and takes off his Confederate officer's hat to show us. And I'll be damned if he didn't have a bullet-sized hole clean through his left lobe.

'Where is he?' the man growls.

'I don't know but that's his sister,' she points to me.

I'd never heard Glonell so articulate. Of course I'd have preferred it if she'd kept her big mouth shut as the man lunged toward me and I am sure I am going to die because he takes my head and squeezes it, python-like, until I nearly lost consciousness – or maybe I did lose consciousness, because the next time I opened my eyes and I'm certain to see the face of the Lord – but it was just Glonell shaking my shoulders and saying, 'wake up, Alice' and when I do she says, 'Hurry – hurry', and I notice her face is spattered in red streaks and droplets all dot and pattern her hands and her white T-shirt. I follow her to the garage where she points to a man behind the back wheel of our mother's Cadillac; and I hear myself whisper: 'Oh my God'.

'He tried to pull my pants down so I hit him with a shovel,' said Glonell.

'You just knocked him out – though – right?'

'No, he dead,' said Glonell.

I looked at the man whose outstretched left arm reached toward nothing ever again, the hand, crumpled and claw-like.

'What did you do that for?' I asked. His skull half-concealed by oily rags now soaking in blood. The ones our father used to wipe off the dipstick in the car's engine.

'Cause I don't want him to see me.'

I had looked under the rags and saw the man's skull was crushed. One eye remained open and stuck fast to the cold cement floor. I told her we had to call the police, and an ambulance. Then I crossed to the other side of the car and proceeded to vomit all over my matching rose-coloured shoes for Mae Lacey's wedding.

'No! The police gonna kick our black ass,' said Glonell. 'Put him outside for the garbage man.'

'Glonell, we have to call the police. Explain to them what happened,' I wiped my mouth. Glonell held her nose while she spoke to me; the sharp sour smell of my vomit and sticky blood filling up the hot garage.

'I'll tell them YOU done it 'cause he gonna hurt ME,' she said.

'I didn't kill him.'

'I save you, Alice,' she said. 'Now you save me.'

I guess I got the idea to give back to the river from my brother. Billy used to say he could see the whole world filter downstream into a great, wide current. Billy gave back to the river stones, and twigs, minnows he caught in an old fruit jar, plus all the loose change jangling around in his twenty-seven pockets.

'Don't you want to keep the money?' I'd ask, hoping he'd give it to me rather than the river.

'No,' he said, 'I don't.'

I pushed the garage-door button and the chains rattled on the metal tracks until it closed and encased us in gloom.

We pulled off the tarp covering old outdoor patio furniture and laid it in the trunk of the car. The general wasn't so tall but he was still heavy. I was afraid Glonell's heart might give trying to lift him but we managed by leaving him jack-knifed against the car, falling across Glonell's back first, then mine – we eventually hauled him in there. I wondered why cousin Raymond needed a pulley system rigged up to lower the body of his girlfriend's ex-boyfriend into his freezer. Why couldn't he just get it over with like me and Glonell? Then I couldn't believe I even thought this. I slammed the trunk shut.

I ran back in the house to get the extra set of car keys. I left a note on the kitchen table:

Gone Fishing
(with Glonell)

And as I backed the car out, I noticed Marvin the dog happily licking the blood and brains and bone off the garage floor.

We hung around the woods until dark and we could hear crickets singing in the low grasses. We filled the pockets of his suit with river rocks. We removed his saddle shoes and dirty socks and buried them under various trees and bushes. He had grown stiff and almost impossible to get out of the trunk. I had to keep inching the car down the boat launch until the back tyres were submerged in river water, then we used clothesline and an old tyre iron we'd found in the trunk and with an unceremonious splash, the current carried a Confederate general somewhere down the crazy river.

ALICE MEETS THE INDIAN

Halfway Island is visible through the cool morning mist that touches the water. In a place where my brother knew the trails and paths as well as any Native American because he had grown up here as a boy, and died here as a man.

The bench I'm on is dedicated to (of all people) Old Lady Sprague for *fifty distinguished years as an educator* – she who drowned in the waters when the river flooded the land.

I never believed Billy's stories about the Indian he mentioned twelve thousand times.

'You're Billy Sycamore's sister,' the man is telling me now more than asking. He's sitting next to me on Mrs Sprague's bench.

'I am.'

'Your brother was a friend of mine.'

'My brother's been dead a long time.'

The Indian is quiet. The early morning shadows cross his cheeks. His eyes intense like flash lightning. There is a huge distance to the man.

You can only travel so far with the dead then you must go back,' said the Indian looking out over the river. The water carries on before us, a great muddy-brown tide travelling between grassy banks and yellow sky. The skeleton of a metal bridge lay half-sunken from the weight of last winter's heavy snows, void and collapsing. The river is happy to have the bridge, claim it as its own. The river does not discriminate. That is the even-hand of it – it will carry you, the river, whoever you are, whatever thoughts you have or don't have, wherever you are from, wherever you happen to be going.

I used to envy the river's indifference. But I don't anymore. I look at him. I hear the muted sounds of flowing water. I used to think that, instead of blood, rivers ran through Billy: streams instead of veins; creeks instead of synapses; tree roots instead of bones. When he had one of his short-term jobs – this one the graveyard shift at 7-11 – he'd let people come in and steal everything. He'd even offer them a shopping bag: *Here. You can carry more tuna.*

Opal Pike cried the loudest at his funeral. Glonell knew somebody was missing but wasn't sure who and our mother swore Billy had come back as a deer, that he rubbed his nose against the kitchen window and jumped in the air, kicking up his legs – *just like he did when he was a little boy running down to the river to go fishing,* she said.

'I loved my brother,' I tell Joseph Lightfoot. I turned away so he wouldn't see my tears.

'Me too,' he said. 'He was a great car salesman.'

And when I looked back, Joseph Lightfoot had flown away like a bird.

THE LAST GARAGE SALE

All year long birds of prey are visible along the Susquehanna River.

Kite, kestrel, and hawk.

There are long fields sloping down, filled with the forgotten seeds of sunflowers. The light shifts, creeping across the face of the mountain. Night and stars hold hands. People sit on their back porches and dream a lot. They eat a hamburger. They turn on the news. They hit their kids. They get promoted. They lose their jobs. They fall in love. They get divorced. They go down to the river to cast in a handful of stones.

Billy's fishing rods sat in a dark corner of our parents' garage. Then our mother had a garage sale. She gave all of Billy's fishing gear to some men from the mental health association of south central Pennsylvania.

They got the blue metallic tackle box, rusting and dented in spots. The black plastic clip that once snapped sharply into place now hung broken and flapping. Next to the box lay a few old copies of *Fly, Rod, & Reel*, *American Angler*, and *The Fish Sniffer*, dog-eared and water-stained. But inside the box remained a delicate, technical, beautiful world. There were flies used to catch steelhead trout and brown mouth bass. There was the Purple Jesus; its body wound with fluorescent pink yarn and its head tied on with red thread. The Royal Wulff was wound with white calf's hair, and the Humpy's tail and wing tied onto a hook with moose hair, sometimes elk.

The men fluttered like butterflies around the box. They seemed to recognise it, knew their way around it: the barbless hooks, the flies and lures, like they'd known Billy, like he was a friend of theirs. Maybe he was.

'Are you sure you don't want any money?' they asked.

'It's all yours,' she smiled, after everything had happened, when it was safe to remember.

There are times in life when it is safe to remember.

---

[1]p14 (from the poem 'Coplas a la Muerte de su Padre' (Stanzas about the Death of his Father) by Spanish poet Jorge Manrique (1440–1479):

Our lives are rivers, gliding free

To that unfathomed, boundless sea,

The silent grave!

ACKNOWLEDGEMENTS

I would like to thank Penny Thomas for her keen eye and ear, grace and patience followed closely by Maura Dooley, Elizabeth Fisher, and Alexandra Shelley, for their own. I would also like to thank Elizabeth Horsley, Heather Steed, and Jacqueline Crooks, Karen Syrett, Brenda Roberts, Francis Fielding, Sandra Goldring, Arthur Krieg, and Isabel O'Neil, all of whom over the days, months, weeks, and years have offered suggestions I could not have done without. I am very grateful to you all.